ELLE GRAY | K.S. GRAY
OLIVIA KNIGHT
FBI MYSTERY THRILLER

THE HOUSEWIFE

The Housewife
Copyright © 2024 by Elle Gray | K.S. Gray

All rights reserved. Without limiting the rights under copyright reserved above, no part of this publication may be reproduced, stored in or intro-duced into retrieval system, or transmitted, in any form, or by any means (electronic, mechanical, photocopying, recording, or otherwise) without the prior written permission of both the copyright owner and the above publisher of this book.

This is a work of fiction. Names, characters, places, brands, media, and in-cidents are either the products of the author's imagination or are used fic-titiously. The author acknowledges the trademarked status and trademark owners of various products referenced in this work of fiction, which have been used without permission. The publication/use of these trademarks is not authorized, associated with, or sponsored by the trademark owners.

PROLOGUE

Kristen Burke's world was a whole lot bigger than it used to be. She had once felt like a small speck on a big planet. Insignificant. Just there to see the world go around. But that had all changed the day she had looked down at a white stick and saw the word *pregnant*. Now, she knew just how important her existence was.

As she walked through the park with her stroller, she looked down at her son as he slept. She'd been told so many times how difficult it would be having a newborn, that it would be a nightmare of sleepless nights and depression and learning how to live all over again. It had worried her so much that she'd spent her entire pregnancy worrying about it, lying awake for hours considering how she would make it all work. She found it ironic now that the pregnancy lost her more sleep than the newborn phase.

Callum was an angel. He slept more than she thought he would, and he didn't spend his waking hours wailing all the time. She had taken him to the pediatrician multiple times, a worried mother just checking that everything was fine, but each time, she had been told that her son was in perfect health. And in moments like this, where he was gently snuffling, his eyes scrunched closed, she truly understood what a gift he was to her. The rest of the world around her might be falling apart, but so long as she was with her son, she felt calm, hopeful, and grateful. He had opened her eyes to how beautiful life could truly be.

But the ugliness of the rest of the world had a way of following her around.

Kristen knew that she was lucky in so many ways, ways that most people would never get to experience. She knew that complaining about her problems out loud would make a lot of people angry. She was the definition of an upper-class woman, and she'd never been anything less. She never had to worry about money—her family's fortune had always kept her comfortable—and she didn't have the pressure of having to work. In fact, unlike her friends who went on to have big, flashy careers, she'd never even had a job. Before Callum was born, her days mostly consisted of yoga classes, beauty appointments, and trips to expensive coffee shops, where she'd idly read or journal, and Tuesday and Thursday afternoons spent planning lavish charity fundraisers—really an excuse to get with the girls and have some drinks and plan opulent parties more than anything approaching "work". Now, looking after the baby had become a full-time job, but it hardly felt like work when it was such a gift. She knew she had no right to complain when there were people all around her struggling to make ends meet, facing the daily struggles of a poor economy and a world crumbling before their eyes. But deeper inside her picture-perfect life, she did have issues of her own. Issues that she may have caused herself, but issues nonetheless.

And no amount of money could fix them.

It was better when she tried not to think about her issues too hard. And that meant avoidance. She took her time walking through the park, though it was getting to be late in the afternoon.

THE **HOUSEWIFE**

Brandon would be home from work soon, and she didn't feel like facing up to him. Things between them had been tense lately. More than usual. She couldn't put her finger on why that was, but it plagued her all the same.

She sighed deeply. Sometimes, she wished she could swap places with her son, to go back to a time when the world was full of wonder and nothing else really mattered. He didn't have to worry about keeping a marriage together, or making irreparable mistakes, or hurting people with cruel words and intentions. And the more she discovered about her husband, the more she wished that she could manipulate time, so maybe she could go back and figure out where it all went wrong.

Eventually, she headed home. She had left her car at home so she would have an excuse to spend longer walking. She told herself it was a good way to lose some of the baby weight, anyway. Maybe if she got back in shape, Brandon would take an interest in her again, despite all they'd been through.

Don't be so hard on yourself, she scolded herself mentally. *Everyone makes mistakes. God knows he does too.* But she knew that she'd struck the first blow. She'd let him down first, and that was the catalyst for everything that had come after. She only had herself to blame. And yet she clung to hope that she could be the one to make it okay again someday.

Callum stayed asleep the whole time, and Kristen focused her thoughts and energy on him. There was no use worrying about what she couldn't control, so she might as well enjoy her time with her son. When she was looking at her beautiful boy, the rest of the world just melted into nothingness around her. Those were the most blissful hours of her life.

"It's you and me against the world, buddy," she whispered under her breath. "We don't need anyone but each other."

It took her a while to reach the gated community where she lived. Brandon often said the place made him feel claustrophobic, like he was trapped in a prison, but it made Kristen feel safe. After all, there were plenty of people who wanted what she had, and she knew there were people out there more than willing to try and steal it all from her. Those gates kept her and her son safe. That was a good enough reason to stay there, despite what Brandon might want. It wasn't that she didn't care about her husband's feelings on the matter, but it was *her* money putting a roof over their head, it was *she* who had labored to give them a child, and now it was *her* job to make sure he never wanted for anything, that he led a safe, secure life. She'd chosen this house with love and care. Brandon might not see it that way, but then again, he always did look for fault in her.

She keyed in the code to the gate and slipped through with the stroller before it was even fully open. Now, her husband was on her mind again. He just didn't understand. He didn't understand that their money was supposed to be a comfort, not something to make him feel suffocated and controlled. He'd insisted on still having a job, though it wasn't necessary at all. That was *his* choice, and she'd allowed him to make it. Sometimes, that did make her feel a little bitter. That was her mother's doing. She'd gotten into her head, making her feel like Brandon was avoiding her. But maybe her mother was right. He *could* be at home spending time with his wife and his child, but these days, she barely saw him. He'd become even more distant throughout her pregnancy and since Callum had been born. He hadn't even taken paternity leave from his job. One weekend, forty-eight hours, was all they had, and then come Monday he was back to work. She couldn't understand why he'd leave her alone that way, why he would keep his distance from his son, but he always seemed to have something more important on his mind. And the more time he spent away from their home, the more Kristen questioned what he was doing with all his spare time.

A road she desperately didn't want to go down.

His car was in the driveway when she got home. She paused on the driveway, feeling a mix of anticipation and nerves. Perhaps today would be better than the day before. Maybe they were slowly, but surely, getting back to how things used to be. Perhaps she just couldn't see it yet, but the progress was coming. If she could only be patient, maybe they'd have a good day someday soon.

She found him in the kitchen, pouring himself a glass of whiskey. He'd always liked a drink, but sometimes she wondered

THE **HOUSEWIFE**

if he was numbing himself every day now, drinking enough to make his mind fuzzy and to push his feelings deep down inside him. Was it his way of shutting her out further?

"Hey, sweetheart," Kristen said, brushing a kiss on her husband's cheek. He didn't return the gesture. He bent briefly to kiss Callum's head before returning to pick up his drink.

"Good day?" Brandon asked Kristen. She tried for a warm smile.

"We went down to that new bakery I've been telling you about."

"Hm?"

"The one on Sheffield? I've been wanting to check it out for ages."

"Oh. Right. I remember," he said, clearly not knowing in the slightest what she was talking about. She pushed past the frustration and only smiled wider.

"And then we had a lovely walk in the park. He's been an angel."

"Good," Brandon said, already walking to the living room. Kristen opened her mouth to say more, but it seemed her husband wasn't interested in having a conversation with her. She prepared to put Callum to bed to continue his nap, and fussed around making dinner in the kitchen. She hoped that Brandon would see the effort and then perhaps he'd look her in the eye. The house felt too quiet these days, when Callum barely had two words to say to her and Brandon even fewer. She almost wished that the baby monitor would go off and that Callum would start crying, just so that she had something to fill her ears. She clattered around the kitchen instead, making as much noise as she could to stave off the silence. After a few minutes, Brandon reappeared in the kitchen. Kristen's face lit up, but his was stormy.

"Will you knock it off? I'm trying to watch something on TV."

Kristen blinked several times. "I'm sorry, I..."

But Brandon was already gone. Kristen leaned against the kitchen counter, feeling herself deflate. Could she do nothing right? She had no idea how she was supposed to fix the discord between them if her husband wasn't interested in making it happen.

Quietly, she continued to make dinner alone.

⁓

A week passed Kristen by. It was Valentine's Day morning and she woke up with a smile on her face. Her husband had promised to be home for dinner that evening, to celebrate the occasion. She hoped it would be the perfect opportunity to rekindle things between them.

She had it all planned out. A new set of lingerie, which she put on beneath her dressing gown as she went about her day. She wanted to feel and look special for him. And then there was dinner—steak was his favorite, so steak it would be. Nothing too fancy, no frills. She'd considered hiring her favorite private chef, but she knew that wasn't the way to go. Brandon preferred to lead an ordinary existence, to act like they weren't filthy rich. She'd never understood why, but she wasn't about to start throwing money around on the day she was hoping to fix things between them. She was a perfectly good cook, she would do it herself.

She fed Callum and changed his diaper before giving the house a quick clean. Then, she set about making Valentine's cookies. She put her earbuds in and blasted the playlist she'd made for her wedding day to Brandon, humming as she measured out the ingredients. *This is going to be a good day,* she told herself, *this is going to be a good day...*

She believed in the power of positivity. It didn't take long for it to take over her. She danced around the kitchen, feeling powerful in her red lingerie. Things were looking up now. Brandon would see the effort she'd put in and then maybe, he would realize he still loved her. It would be a lovely dinner and an even more lovely night, once the baby was put to bed.

She smiled to herself so wide she almost missed the shadow moving across the kitchen.

She frowned and turned around to look for what had caused it, but she couldn't see anything. She shook her head. She still felt

THE **HOUSEWIFE**

like she had a baby brain from time to time. She must've imagined it.

She arranged the cookies on the baking tray and slid them into the oven. She stood at the counter for a while, listening to her music and allowing the aroma of the baking to fill her nose. With her timer ticking away, she knew she could go and get on with other things, maybe check in on Callum, but there was a quiet calmness to the moment that she felt like savoring. *Everything is going to get better,* she told herself.

Brrrrring!

She blinked and returned to the moment. Had ten minutes passed so quickly? It felt like there was only one.

She bent to open up the oven and sniffed deeply of the deep, warm sweetness of the sugar cookies, when she felt a presence behind her. She smiled, and for good measure, stuck out her butt and wriggled it back and forth in what she hoped was an alluring way.

"Someone's home early for some sugar," she purred.

She pulled the sheet out of the oven and rose back to her full height, but the moment she turned around, she dropped it to the floor with a resounding clang.

A hand clamped over her mouth before she had a chance to scream.

CHAPTER ONE

"Read it," Brock said, thrusting the piece of paper straight at Olivia. "Read what Yara has to say for herself. After all this time, and she sends this..."

Olivia took the piece of paper a little shakily. It had been months since they'd heard from Yara Montague——the disgraced actress and Brock's close friend——since she was broken out of prison along with the infamous Gamemaster, Adeline Clarke. Olivia had no idea how Yara had managed to get in touch with them or why, but curious as she was, she almost didn't want to read the letter. They hadn't spoken to Yara since she had betrayed them back on the Gamemaster's island. They'd had the choice to visit her before her trial, but Brock had immediately declined. Yara wasn't the person they thought she was. She was a killer and

THE **HOUSEWIFE**

a liar and a danger to them all. Granted, it was her addiction and desperation to live that had driven her to do such awful things, but Olivia hadn't forgotten what she had done, and Brock certainly hadn't. She glanced at Brock, her face soft.

"Is it a good idea to read this? Whatever it is, it can't be good."

"Well, I've read it, so now you'll have to. I need to know what you think," Brock said, anxiety crossing his handsome face. When Brock was taking something seriously, Olivia knew it had to be important. There was no trace of his usual jovial self. Olivia turned her attention to the letter, taking a steadying deep breath. She supposed there was nothing to do, but dive right in.

To Olivia and Brock,

I am sorry it has taken me so long to get in contact with you. Fear has stopped me from trying to speak to you. Not just fear for myself, but fear of what might happen to you if I encourage you to find me… and The Gamemaster. But I know now that I must, no matter the cost to myself. And I know you can handle yourselves. You have proved that enough times.

I promise you, this letter is no trick. I have tried everything to try and escape myself. I have been beaten and bullied into submission with each attempt. I am too weak to save myself, and now I have to appeal to you to end this thing once and for all.

I cannot speak plainly, in case this letter is found by the wrong people and our location is changed. But we are at a place that is hidden in plain sight. You could pass us on the street, but you would never see us. Times are tough, but time has become our friend. If you look too hard, you will not find us. If you don't look at all, we'll be right behind you.

I hope that is enough. I hope you find us. I will happily return to prison to serve out my sentence. I only want The Gamemaster to be caught and brought to justice. I know I don't deserve freedom, and I swear to you, I had no idea that I would be rescued from that van. I've made many, many mistakes, but I never wanted things to turn out this way.

I know you hate me right now. I know you don't believe you can trust me, and maybe you can't. Some days, I don't even trust myself.

I'm not the person I once was. My vices have me in a chokehold. But I hope this message finds you safe. I hope you figure it all out. I hope you come looking for me. And I hope you come fast.

I don't know what comes next. I don't know what The Gamemaster has planned. But I fear that she will use me somehow. It's been months now, and I don't know why she would keep me around unless she had some use for me. And I don't want to be a piece in her games again.

Signed,
Yara Montague

Olivia exhaled loudly, folding the letter back in half. It was going to take her a little while to process what she'd just read. Brock studied her, his brow creased as he tried to read her expression.

"Well? What do you think? It's crazy, right?"

Olivia shook her head in disbelief. Crazy was one word for it. It wasn't exactly usual to get letters like that in the mail. But Olivia had learned long ago that nothing about her life with Brock was ordinary. It took quite a lot to shock her now.

But the letter had shaken her, for sure.

"I have no idea. The timing is... strange. She's had months to get in contact. Why now? I know she said she's been biding her time, but it just feels off. And the riddle she left us for her location... it doesn't seem like something that Yara would write."

"That's what I thought. She's not one for riddles. But we know who it is."

"The Gamemaster," Olivia murmured. She had not forgotten their first task on the Gamemaster's desert island. They had to solve riddles or die trying. The game claimed the life of one of their group, the first to die on the island. The Gamemaster had happily watched it all happen. How could they not think of that terrible week when they were presented with a riddle now?

"This has to be a trick," Brock said, shaking his head. "The Gamemaster is trying to draw us out, to try and get us to play a game again. This is probably happening now because she's been busy planning all of this time. We can't bite."

Olivia chewed her lip. "Except..."

"Olivia, no. We can't start believing that this is anything but a trick. Then the Gamemaster wins."

"But even if it's a trick, it's likely that Yara is in danger. She wouldn't let her go. She's her leverage, after all. She's your friend..."

"She *was* my friend."

"Brock, I know you still care about her. It's your weakness and The Gamemaster knows it too. But I guess she didn't count on you dismissing the letter without a second thought."

Brock sighed. "Well, of course I still care. But I'm not about to be lured in. The Gamemaster is a threat to the entire country, and to us in particular. I'm sure she wants us dead after we managed to unmask her and put her behind bars. And not to mention the fact that Yara is a liar too. The Gamemaster could've been using this time to corrupt her, to make her write this letter and lure us in. What else does she have to lose? The Gamemaster is probably keeping her from being sober, torturing her, forcing her to be on her side."

Olivia knew that Brock was talking sense. They were dealing with an incredibly twisted individual. The Gamemaster knew no bounds when it came to manipulation, so long as the outcome was shocking for her audience. That's how she had gained her fame long before she forced ten people onto the island to compete for their lives.

But Olivia wanted to believe that Yara had some decency left over inside her. Brock was usually a good judge of character, and he'd chosen her as his friend. He'd even briefly dated her as a younger man, so how could he be so wrong about a person? Yara was good at heart. She was just troubled. Could she really be manipulated to help the Gamemaster a second time? After having to live with the guilt of everything she'd done the first time around?

Olivia rubbed at her temple. The letter had thrown them a curveball, that was for sure. Just when they were beginning to put their ordeal in the past, this new dilemma had shown up. How were they supposed to handle it? Could they just ignore it? Olivia didn't believe so. As FBI agents, a letter like this couldn't be forgotten.

"I don't think we can ignore this," she told Brock. "It's not about how we feel about Yara or the matter at hand. We haven't heard a peep from the Gamemaster in months. Trick or not, this is coming from her camp. This is our chance to track her down. But we can do it on our own terms. Decode the letter and figure out what it means. I mean, the riddle alone... it's complicated, but it's not particularly coherent. I think maybe Yara could've written it, given the wording of it. And if she really is reaching out for help, are we willing to leave her out in the cold?"

"She'd do the same to us," Brock murmured, but Olivia could tell his heart wasn't in it. He did care, whether he wanted to admit it or not. And if this was their chance to get Yara to safety, then Olivia was sure he wouldn't turn it down, even after everything she had said and done.

"We will have to talk to Jonathan about this," Olivia said. "But maybe not yet."

"You want to keep this from him?"

"Not exactly. But you know the pressure this case put on him. He won't say it, but it almost broke him. I don't know what she did to him before we arrived on that boat, but he hasn't been the same since. I think we should take a few days to try and figure out the riddle for ourselves before we talk to him. I mean, what's all this stuff about hiding in plain sight? She said if we don't look, they'll be right behind us. Does that mean they're keeping tabs on us? And she mentions time twice... *times are tough, but time has become our friend.* Is she trying to imply that we need to be fast? That they've been biding their time and that something is about to happen, maybe?"

Brock considered it. "It's possible. If time is their friend, then they think they have the upper hand. But I don't know... is that a little basic?"

"That depends on whether we're talking to Yara or the Gamemaster here. I don't know. It's a lot to take in."

Brock took the letter from Olivia's hand and tucked it into his pocket. "I think we need to sleep on this. We've only just arrived home. We're not thinking straight. We can revisit this in the morning."

THE **HOUSEWIFE**

Olivia's eyes softened. "We can't run from this, Brock. You know that, right?"

Brock pulled Olivia close to him, resting his chin on the top of her head. "I know. But just for one night, let me pretend that we can. Let me pretend that we're normal."

Olivia knew that they'd never be normal, but she didn't say that out loud. She held him back, her hands balling his shirt into her fists. She tilted her chin up to look at Brock, searching his face for emotion, but he closed the gap to kiss her instead. She allowed it, kissing him back with an urgency that surprised even herself. She wasn't one for escapism, but where Brock was concerned, it was easy to get lost in him and forget the rest of the world.

Even if everything they knew was on fire.

CHAPTER TWO

A few months later...

"**D**O WE HAVE TO GO TO THIS THING?" Olivia complained as she pulled on her jacket, pouting her lip. Brock grinned at her.

"You'd think it was me dragging *you* to *my* high school reunion, not the other way around. Don't be anti-social, Olivia. It'll be fun."

Olivia rolled her eyes with a smile. It was true that it was her reunion, but that didn't mean she was exactly looking forward to

THE **HOUSEWIFE**

it. Brock knew her well enough to know it was her own personal idea of hell. High school seemed like such a long time ago to her, and she hadn't kept in touch with many of the people who she went there with. She hadn't been unpopular, but she also hadn't been one of the best-loved students. She wasn't the one who got invited to every party and got asked to prom by every guy in class. She was just ordinary.

Her life was very different now, of course. Becoming an FBI agent was the best thing she'd ever decided to do. The issue was that it tended to encourage a lot of unwanted attention at reunions and the like. The moment anyone discovered where her career path had taken her, it was all anyone wanted to talk about. It made Olivia feel awkward and boastful, though she didn't like to show off about her job. Half the people at the reunion would love her for it, and the other half would treat her with bitter disdain, either jealous of how life turned out for her or with outright suspicion that she'd chosen to go into law enforcement at all. It was like being back at high school itself, with a hierarchy of people fighting for power and social status. It didn't appeal to her in the slightest. That's why she was dreading going now, though she had accepted the invitation without much hesitation at the time. She was almost tempted to tell people that she worked at the local grocery store instead to avoid the conversation entirely.

"Well, I guess this is a mess of my own making," Olivia said, fetching her purse from the coffee table. "But if it's a total nightmare, do you promise you'll take me straight home? I'm not in the mood to deal with anything too wild tonight."

"You won't be saying that after the first tequila."

"There will be *no* tequila tonight."

"That's what you always say until your nerves get the better of you. Then you're reaching for the lime and the salt and I'm silently planning how to carry you home without making too much of a scene."

Olivia tutted at Brock's tall tale and swatted him with her purse as he scurried for the door. "Get out, troublemaker. You've never once done that. You're the one always staggering out of bars after three beers…"

He gave his trademark grin. "I'm a party boy at heart. Old age won't stop me."

Olivia chuckled as she stepped out after Brock and locked the door. She double-checked the lock, a brief squeeze of anxiety seizing her heart. In recent months, caution had taken over her again. With the Gamemaster still on the run and Yara's letter constantly at the back of her mind, she didn't leave the house much except for work. She felt it was for the best, with a constant threat hanging over their heads. But nothing had happened since they received the letter. They'd tried to decode it numerous times, but they were yet to succeed. But Olivia often thought about one line from the letter. *If you look too hard, you will not find us. If you don't look at all, we'll be right behind you.* It was an ominous statement. She found herself constantly looking over her shoulder, as though they might just appear behind her at any point. It wasn't an easy way to live her life, but it felt all too familiar to her.

Olivia was fully aware that her anxieties got her nowhere. Double-checking her locks wouldn't stop the Gamemaster if she wanted to enter her home. It wouldn't be the first time she had been robbed or had her house broken into. But it gave her the slightest amount of relief, and it was the only thing that got her into Brock's car and heading toward her hometown for the reunion. She was quiet for most of the journey, mulling things over in her head. How was she meant to concentrate on anything as ordinary as a high school reunion when their entire life was a never-ending puzzle, designed to test them to their very limits? It made her feel just about as far as she could be from an ordinary life.

But a different kind of anxiety took over as they neared the bar that was hosting the reunion. She was perfectly socially capable, and yet it felt strange to spend the night with a bunch of people who had once been acquaintances, but now were strangers. She wondered why people did it to themselves. Why she had done it to herself, for that matter. But as they parked, she spied a few familiar faces. Faces of people who had never left the little town of Melrose, who had squeezed into their letterman jackets for the occasion and were now laughing a little too loud and drinking

THE **HOUSEWIFE**

beers together. They all seemed perfectly at ease. She guessed that not much had changed for them in the time she'd been away. Olivia took a steadying breath.

"You okay?" Brock asked. She smiled.

"Sure I am. Let's do this before I chicken out."

The pair of them got out of the car and headed toward the bar. Olivia kept her arms wrapped around herself, suddenly self-conscious of her plain black pants and her white blouse. Did she dress too old for her age? Had she grown up too fast? Everyone around her seemed to be stuck in the past, not looking like they had changed much since they left high school fifteen years before. Her life had transformed a hundred times since then. She had thought that was part of growing up. But perhaps that was just the turbulence of her own life talking. Not everyone had to endure the things she had. And she was glad of it. She was glad to see her old classmates happy, even if she felt like a fish out of water among them.

The bar was stuffy and hot after the coldness outside. As Olivia entered the room, every face seemed to turn to see who was arriving next. Olivia's eyes skittered over the guests. A group of the popular girls from school bent their faces close to one another's, whispering about her arrival. Her first ever boyfriend, Gareth Timms, was standing at the bar and raised a beer to her with a wink. Others clocked her and turned away in disinterest, clearly hoping for someone more exciting. She rolled her eyes internally. *Some things never change.* Maybe she didn't have to worry about people taking too much interest in her after all.

Olivia looked around for someone that she would be happy to talk to, but the more she searched, the less comfortable she felt. Had anyone she knew even turned up? She was almost tempted to turn around and head back outside when she saw a group standing at the far end of the bar, laughing and talking. Olivia's heart lifted.

She had forgotten a few of the people who were standing with the group, but there were three of them who stood out to her; Louis Cane, the jokester she'd sat next to in algebra class for three straight years, Jules Matthews, the sweet posh girl from England,

and Emma Phillips, the super-cool rebel girl who used to challenge all of the teachers. She sported a bunch of face piercings and a smattering of tattoos now, which Olivia had somehow expected, but otherwise she hadn't changed a bit. Olivia smiled and set her sights on their group. If she was going to feel comfortable anywhere, it would be with them and their familiarity.

Louis spotted her first and his face lit up in a grin. He waved her over enthusiastically, drawing the attention of the others at the table. He stepped up to give her a bone-crushing hug.

"Well, well, well… if it isn't Olivia Knight!" he declared.

"In the flesh," she replied. "Good to see you. It's been too long."

"It would have been less time if you had social media like a normal person," he needled. "Come on, I'll buy you a beer. You remember Jules, don't you? And of course, Emma Phillips! Or should I say… Emma *Cane?*"

Olivia's mouth fell open as Emma rolled her eyes and greeted her with a quick hug.

"Yeah, I don't know what I was thinking either," Emma said sarcastically, but there was a smile tugging at the corner of her lips as Louis threaded an arm around her slim waist. Olivia found herself laughing.

"I can't believe you got married. I never would have paired you together! At least not back then…"

"Emma likes to tell everyone that I fell first, but let's be real. She couldn't get enough of this," Louis said with a grin, gesturing his hands down his torso. "And who is this handsome fella you've brought with you? The dish of the day?"

"I like this guy," Brock said, offering a hand for him to shake. "Brock Tanner. I'm Olivia's partner. In life and in work."

"A workplace romance? Oh, you *must* spill the beans," Jules insisted, her accent as fruity as Olivia remembered. "There's nothing more juicy than that. What is it that you do?"

Olivia and Brock exchanged a glance and a smile. Olivia had known the question would come up at some point, but she thought she might have a little time to relax first. She took a deep breath, ready to make her reveal.

"We're FBI agents."

THE **HOUSEWIFE**

A collective 'oooh' went around the table and Olivia had to hold back a nervous giggle. She was soon being bombarded with questions about her work, about her most gristly cases and about her most exciting experiences. Olivia almost didn't notice as a small crowd of her previous classmates gathered around to listen to her tales. Brock stuck close to her side, his hand on her hip, and Olivia swore she saw some of the women eyeing him up. He was almost as much of a hit as her career seemed to be among her peers. But her pride in her partner equally matched her pride in her work. Having Brock there beside her made her feel luckier than she could ever truly express.

There was plenty to talk about, at least. She would never run out of things to say. She told them about moving to Belle Grove and how trouble seemed to follow her there. She explained how she had met Brock and the pair of them were soon inseparable, often investigating shocking cases among the rich and famous. She told them about the cults they'd taken down, about the crazed serial killers they'd stopped, about the massive international conspiracies they'd shut down. She told them all about The Gamemaster, and many of her peers were shocked to learn of her involvement in such a big case. Nearly all of them had heard about it on the news, but she was glad that no one had watched the livestream.

After a while, Olivia began to feel a little claustrophobic with all the questions, and she insisted that she had to get a drink. Though her peers seemed to want to hear more, they soon moved on to talk among themselves. As she and Brock headed to the bar, she hoped that upon her return, the topic would switch over to someone else and she'd be able to fade into the background again. As she ordered herself a beer, she took a deep breath and Brock smiled at her.

"Looks like somebody is the star of the show," he teased. She rolled her eyes.

"I should've known this would happen."

"You're telling me you're not interested in being the center of attention in the slightest?"

"No, I'm not! I'm not *you*," Olivia said pointedly. "I came here for a catch-up, not to perform a one-woman show. I want to catch up with gossip, compare school dynamics to now, all that stuff…"

"Well you shouldn't be so damn interesting then," Brock said, kissing the side of Olivia's face. She raised an eyebrow at him.

"Well, I'm not the only thing drawing attention… you do realize you're the trophy wife of the night?"

Brock spluttered with laughter. "What are you talking about?"

"Brock, you're easily the best-looking man in the room. Plus you've got an interesting job, you're likable, you're funny… you're making me look good. And every woman—plus a few guys—have their eyes on you."

Brock chuckled. "Don't forget my beautiful eyes and my rock-hard abs."

Olivia nudged him with her elbow. "Shut up."

He feigned shock and pretended to fall over. "Ow! You know, if you keep treating me like this, you'd better hope I don't get a better offer tonight and get whisked away by someone else…"

"Oh, I'm not too worried. They'd bring you right back to me when they realize how irritating you are."

Brock laughed loudly and Olivia grinned back. She loved nothing more than to be reminded of exactly why she was with Brock in the first place. He brought out the best in her. The side of her that knew how to take a joke, to not take life too seriously. It felt nice to be reminded of the early days when their relationship seemed so easy. The past few months had taken a toll on both of them with Yara's letter looming like a dark cloud over their lives. Their love had never faltered, but sometimes, their individual strength had. But just for tonight, it didn't feel like an issue. It felt like something that could be left to simmer in the background, if only for a while.

Olivia and Brock returned to the group to find Louis loudly telling the story of how he'd run back into Emma in college and embarked on a calculated, exacting campaign of romantic intention—which Emma saw through immediately, and proceeded to tease and torture him about until she somehow found herself catching feelings as well. Olivia was more than

THE **HOUSEWIFE**

happy to listen, laughing along with his dumb jokes and Emma's sarcastic quips. It took the pressure off for a while, and she was glad of someone else taking the spotlight. She was pleased for them. How differently their lives had turned out——Emma and Louis were expecting their second child, and they both worked in marketing and graphic design, a far cry from Olivia's own situation. And yet, their lives had so many quirks she could never dream of, so much excitement in their family antics that Olivia had yet to experience. As the night drew on, she found herself comparing herself to others. It was easy to get caught up in everyone's tales, to see how they might be doing things that Olivia hadn't gotten to try yet. Jules spent a good while telling her about how she split her time between England and New York, where she owned multiple properties inherited from her rich father. Olivia's last trip to the UK had been something of a disaster, so she couldn't find herself relating to the stories, though she did envy Jules' ability to relax.

"Sometimes, you just have to get away, don't you?" she said as she concluded her story about holidaying in Mauritius after her childhood dog died. "I am grateful that I have the freedom to just get up and leave. I suppose I always knew working life wasn't for me… I may have attended public school, but I grew far too used to my creature comforts. I am *so* fortunate to be able to travel whenever I please…"

"That must be lovely," Olivia said honestly, wondering what it would be like if she had unlimited money and time off work to see the world. Jules' life was one she would never have, but she didn't find herself overly jealous. She found herself rich in other ways. The thought crossed her mind as she glanced at Brock. She had to hide her smile.

"Perhaps you should come over to England with me sometime. You would all be *so* welcome at my cottage in the Cotswolds," Jules gushed. "Sally came with me a few months ago… you remember Sally Perry, don't you?" Jules said, pulling a woman by her arm into the conversation. Olivia didn't remember her one bit, not even after seeing her face. The woman in front of her was pretty, but not stunningly so. She had a brown bob that was a little too old for her age, and like Olivia, she had dressed smartly for the occasion. Olivia didn't want to admit that the woman seemed like a total stranger to her, so she smiled pleasantly and nodded.

"Of course I do. How are you, Sally?"

"Good, thanks," Sally said, offering a quick smile. She didn't return the question. "What are we talking about?"

"Oh… Jules was just telling me that you went to her house in the Cotswolds to visit."

"All expenses paid," Jules added with a smug smile. Olivia had to stop herself from cringing. Sally looked equally uncomfortable.

"Yeah, we've traveled together a couple of times. It's nice to take a break every now and then."

"Where do you work?" Brock asked, steering the conversation.

"Oh, nothing as interesting as being in the FBI," Sally said with a short laugh. She kept her voice level and Olivia couldn't tell whether she was being aggressive toward her. "I work in closets."

"Oh, wow! In fashion design? I remember you being arty at school, right?" Olivia said, hoping that she had made a correct guess. Sally's forehead creased.

"No, I work in closet renovations. I'm just an assistant to the CEO. And no, not really. I've never been much of an artist. I work to pay the bills, that's all."

"Well, I think that's the way to go," Brock said with a smile. "Might as well enjoy our time on Earth. We only get one shot at it."

"Hear, hear!" Jules said, raising her glass. "A toast! To old friends and to enjoying life!"

"I can drink to that!" Olivia said, smiling at Sally. There was a moment's hesitation before Sally clinked her glass against Olivia's.

"Good to see you again, Olivia," Jules said as they all took a drink. "Let's hope it's not another decade-plus before we meet up again!"

Olivia felt the night slip quickly past her in a pleasant blur. She spoke to as many people as she could, making the rounds of everyone, even the girls who had whispered when she arrived. And all too soon, it was time to leave. She had arrived at the event feeling like it was the last place she wanted to be, but she left with a handful of phone numbers and promises to stay in touch.

THE **HOUSEWIFE**

Louis and Emma insisted on inviting Olivia to their upcoming wedding, and Jules asked Olivia to join her and Sally on their trip to Amsterdam. The feeling of the evening made Olivia feel light and airy as she and Brock walked back to the car.

"Good night?" Brock asked. Olivia nodded enthusiastically.

"A really good night. I think I needed it."

Brock squeezed her hand. "I think we both did."

The pair of them slid into the car and Brock started up the engine. "So… do you think you'll be making that trip to Amsterdam?"

Olivia laughed. "I doubt it. But it was nice to be asked. It's weird… I used to be so jealous of Jules and her expensive lifestyle… but I guess I'm content with the way things are. I didn't feel this urge to jet set off with her like Sally does…"

"Well, I imagine Sally's job doesn't stimulate her as much as ours does," Brock said. "Not that there's anything wrong with that. But I suppose she has a rich friend keeping her busy, doesn't she?"

"True… and that's nice, in a weird way. Everyone in that room was living such different lives. Some of them were doing things I never imagined that they would, but most of them seemed so happy, right? And not like they were pretending to be happy. Like they really loved their life. That's such a lovely thing."

Brock patted Olivia's knee. "Exactly. And yet I think we were the happiest of them all."

CHAPTER THREE

When Olivia's phone rang promptly at six in the morning one mid-February day, she knew immediately who would be calling. Only her boss, Special Agent in Charge Jonathan James ever had the urge to call her at such an hour. It was fortunate that she had already been awake, lying quietly beside Brock to enjoy the peace of the morning. Now, she quietly slid out of bed, not wanting to wake Brock yet, and took the call in the living room.

"Good morning. Nice to hear from you bright and early," Olivia said with a yawn. "Are we still on for brunch?"

"I've got a case for you," Jonathan said, getting straight to the point. He didn't tend to have time for niceties or chit-chat.

THE **HOUSEWIFE**

"A young, rich woman from Melrose has been killed in her own home on Valentine's Day."

"Oh," Olivia said.

"Her husband came home to the smell of burning and found that she had been stabbed numerous times in her kitchen. She was caught off guard, the oven was still on as she'd been baking. Their child was unharmed, but left alone for a number of hours upstairs in his crib. But what's interesting is that the woman in question, Kristen Burke, lived in a gated community."

"So presumably a lot of security to get through, right?"

"Correct. The gate itself needs a code to enter the neighborhood, and then she had a pretty substantial security system in her own home as well. According to her husband's report, she had concerns for her family's safety, given that they were quite wealthy. She had security cameras fitted on the exterior, though something tells me that whoever did this will have disabled them. And this is no ordinary killing. There's more."

"There is?"

"A number of expensive things were missing from the home when the body was found. I haven't been given a full inventory, but I believe a number of expensive personal effects were among the stolen items——handbags and jewelry among them."

"So, a break-in gone wrong?"

"Perhaps. But from my understanding, the robbery seemed only secondary to the killer's primary purpose—the murder itself. The Melrose Police Department has requested our assistance as they deal with the residents of the gated community to ensure their safety."

"Ah, I see. The Richie Riches put their thumbs on the scale to send the Feds out there, then?"

Jonathan only made a *hrm*, neither confirming nor denying it. "Our killer was bold enough to strike in broad daylight and capable of completely bypassing some of the finest security systems on the market. My guess is that they will strike again, and probably soon. That's why I want you and Brock on the case. I believe you're the best hope we have of getting this handled, quickly and quietly."

"Money sure talks, doesn't it?"

He didn't reply to this quip, either. "The residents in the community have been taken somewhere safe until this blows over, but it's a rich area in general. Melrose is full of similar houses and that makes for a lot of potential contacts. I imagine that if there are more hits, they will be close by. Perhaps the killer will strike a few times and then flee the area and try somewhere else. We need to try and move with some urgency if we're going to get this one."

"Understood. I'll wake Brock and we'll get going."

"Good. Keep me posted, and good luck."

When Olivia returned to her bedroom, Brock was already out of bed and getting dressed. He was no early bird, so Olivia assumed the sound of her accepting a case had been enough to get him out of bed. He smiled at her.

"He's not joining us for brunch, is he?"

Olivia chuckled silently. "I made the same joke. No, he's got other plans. Paperwork to fill out, you know—assigning out murder cases."

"Oh, well, that doesn't mean he can't stop by for some pancakes."

"Brock..."

"Come on. Can't solve a murder on an empty stomach."

Olivia sighed. "Sure, I guess we can start out at the diner before heading out to the scene. But we'll have to make it quick."

"We can take it to go, if you don't mind me spilling maple syrup on the seats..."

She headed to the closet to pull out some clothes. "Someone's in a hurry to get started on work. You don't even know what the case is."

"I don't need to. I'm ready for anything. We spend way too much time on paperwork lately. Give me something to sink my teeth into."

Olivia suppressed a sigh. Over the last six months, Brock's dedication to work had leveled up, but she knew it was mostly just a distraction for him. A distraction from Yara and her letters, from the horrors they left behind on the island. She'd sent another few

THE **HOUSEWIFE**

over the past couple of months, crying out for help, trying to tug Olivia and Brock back into the mystery of what had happened to her. It had only been two days since the last desperate letter. They still hadn't decoded the first one and their apparent location, but Yara hadn't suggested that they'd moved.

It had been decided by Jonathan that it was best to let someone else handle Yara's case, knowing that Olivia and Brock were too close to the situation. When they'd handed the first letter over to him, he'd promised to put some of his best agents onto the task, but they too hadn't discovered anything as of yet. In some ways, Olivia was glad. The further she and Brock kept from it all, the better.

But Olivia thought about the letter often. Sometimes at night, she'd lie awake wondering what Yara's words had meant, whether they came from her at all, whether she really was trying to help them catch the Gamemaster. She wondered if Yara lay awake too, consumed by the guilt of everything she'd done to survive the island.

But every time, she'd fall asleep with more questions than answers. Yara was a complex woman, and she'd fooled them once before. The woman Olivia thought she'd come to know was the same one who kidnapped her and took her to face the Gamemaster on the boat. She was the same woman who had spent a week playing on her side, only for Olivia to find out that she'd killed one of the members of their group. That wasn't something she was about to forget in a hurry. It made Olivia feel like she didn't know who she could trust.

But with Brock at her side, she knew at least one person she could rely on.

As soon as the two of them were ready, they headed off—to-go boxes of breakfast and all. Melrose was a couple hours away, so they had to drive through Washington, DC to get there. Olivia scrolled through some photos of the picturesque town and her eyebrows rose high on her head.

"Well, Jonathan wasn't wrong. This town looks fancy," she said. Brock shook his head.

"Why is it that we spend half our time running around after rich people? They're always getting themselves in trouble. If I was that loaded, I think I'd take myself off to somewhere quiet where no one could find me. Then I'd never have to deal with all this stuff."

"Easier said than done. I think the Earth's running out of habitable private islands," Olivia said sarcastically.

As they continued the drive and Brock concentrated on the road, Olivia wasn't thinking much about the case they were about to embark on. It was Yara on her mind, and their most recent letter from her that had arrived two days earlier.

To Olivia and Brock,

I don't know if these letters are making it to you, but if they are, please don't ignore me. I know I don't deserve your help, but even if you don't do this for me, do it for the country. The Gamemaster is dangerous, more dangerous than I ever anticipated. I'm scared of what she might do next. She's planning something big, something that will wreak havoc across the country. Only you can save us from this.

Please. Please don't shut me out.

Yara

"Olivia?"

"Hmm?"

"You're in a world of your own."

"Sorry... I was just thinking."

"I know what's on your mind," Brock said, his tone masking frustration. "But you can't let it swallow you whole. Yara isn't in our hands anymore. It's someone else's case."

"I know. But this is so personal. She keeps reaching out to us..."

"We still don't know that. The Gamemaster wants us vulnerable. She wants to appeal to our emotions. This would be the perfect way to do it. She knows that we're the only people left who might care about what happens to Yara."

"I know... but you know what Jonathan told us. The handwriting matches previous samples of Yara's writing."

"So the Gamemaster forced her to write it. Or she did it willingly because she works with her now, I don't know. Either way, how can this be anything other than a trap? How do you think Yara could sneak away to send these letters without being caught? It's just not possible for someone like her to trick someone like the Gamemaster. She isn't smart enough for that. The more letters we receive, the more convinced I am that it's all a ruse."

Olivia sighed. Brock's cynicism had only grown in recent times. He had no reason to trust Yara after what she had done, of course, but it was as though he had forgotten the person she was before. As though that person had been wiped clean from the slate when she snapped and worked with the Gamemaster. It was like he couldn't consider the reasons she had done everything she had done, driven to madness by her own illness. Where Olivia could find sympathy, Brock had grown cold and angry.

Olivia understood. She understood all too well how easy it was to hate someone you cared about deep down. She'd been betrayed enough times, after all. But she wished sometimes that he didn't see the world in such a black and white way. She knew there was more to the story if he was just willing to open his eyes to it.

But he was a stubborn man. That hadn't changed in the time she had known him. He'd need a pretty good reason to change his mind now, to even agree to wanting Yara back safely, even if it was in a prison cell. Olivia took a deep breath, wondering how to approach the tricky subject again.

"You don't have to like her. You don't have to care what happens to her. But if we're being involved by Yara or the Gamemaster... then it's not something we can run away from. We're being drawn into this whether we like it or not, and it's our duty to try and get to the bottom of it. It's our duty to try and get Yara out alive, if we can."

"She's not some innocent bystander, Olivia. She *killed* someone. She tried to kill both of us. She aided the Gamemaster with her plans, and that makes her complicit. She was going to prison for life anyway. Her life was over the moment she made the decision to help the Gamemaster. Her only chance at freedom now is to do her bidding and live outside of the law. In her shoes, what would you do?"

"I don't know what I'd do…"

"Well, I can guess what she'd do. She's already killed someone to escape her own fate. If it's a choice between a prison cell for life or a dangerous life on the run, I think she's going to pick the latter, don't you? At least she'll go down with a thrill."

"Brock…"

"I don't know why we keep fighting on her behalf. It's not like she would do that for anyone, is it?"

"That was never her job. But it is ours."

Brock remained silent, his hands tight on the steering wheel. Olivia wished sometimes that she could read his mind. Did he really not care at all about what would happen to his former friend? Olivia was still hoping to see her again, safe and sound, even after everything. She hoped that the flicker of regret she'd seen in her on the boat would still live on inside her, fueling her to choose the right path this time. Maybe she'd redeem herself. Maybe she was trying to by warning them about what was to come.

But she guessed that was only because she only saw Yara as she was now—not as the woman she'd once been. She didn't have years of friendship with Yara behind her. Though she still recalled how Yara took her down, how she ignored her pleas as she escorted her to the Gamemaster, she somehow couldn't take it entirely personally. It took far too much strength to disobey an order when you were fighting for your life, Olivia felt. Yara was manipulated and used, nothing more.

But Brock didn't see it that way.

Brock ran a hand through his hair, sighing deeply.

"Look, I understand where you're coming from, Olivia. I know that it feels close to home, because it is. We're being singled out, constantly reminded of what happened back on the island, of what we went through with Yara. But I think that's how we're being *forced* to feel. And for me, it's just easier to wipe the slate clean and pretend like this woman that we supposedly knew… it's easier to pretend she's a stranger. That she's entirely separate from the Yara I knew. In my mind, I tell myself that a woman died on the island, because she's not the same as the one who is on the run with the Gamemaster now. It's not that I don't care. Despite myself, I do. But I want nothing to do with the investigation. I don't even want to talk about it. Which is why I… I've kept back some of the letters."

"Brock! I thought we agreed to hand everything over to Jonathan!"

"I know… but I guess I didn't want to draw anyone further into this mess. We could've died on that island, Olivia. People did. And whatever the Gamemaster is up to, it's going to put people in danger once again. And I don't want to be responsible for that. It's too much. So I guess I thought I was keeping people safe by keeping the letters. There's nothing in them that isn't covered in the first letter anyway. But… but if I really want to wash my hands of this, then I suppose it's time to let the letters go. I'll send them to Jonathan and the team he has on the case. And then from there… I'm done."

Olivia felt like she wanted to argue with him, to try and make him see it from another point of view, but she stopped herself. She knew there was nothing she could say that would make Brock feel differently, and now she saw that it might be better that way. He was right. Keeping their distance from Yara's case was the safest route. But as she let the topic slide with Brock, it didn't leave her mind. Something told her that choosing to turn their back on the Gamemaster wasn't an option. She would be the one who decided whether they played or not. They had already become her fixation once, and she doubted they would be let off the hook so easily.

But one good thing came from the conversation. Olivia watched Brock and saw how much he had grown as a man. His choice to let Yara go showed his growing maturity. He knew what he wanted, and it wasn't to spend his entire life entangled in a mess he wasn't able to solve. It had taken her a lot longer than him to know her own mind, to not let the trauma of her past cloud her judgment.

Perhaps Olivia had hoped he would respond differently, but she was glad that Brock was closer to his old self now. He'd learned to live life again——to smile, to laugh, to try and leave the past where it belonged. What happened on the island had brought him to his breaking point, and yet he'd survived it. If he was coming back even stronger now, resilient against even the hardest scenarios, then she had to feel proud of him for it.

Life wasn't perfect. In a perfect world, Yara never would've put Brock in such a position in the first place. In a perfect world, there would be no bad guys to catch and they'd be out of a job, but they'd be without turmoil too.

But Olivia had accepted long ago that turbulence was a part of the life they led. She'd also accepted that sometimes, the answer wasn't simple. If letting go of this whole thing was the only thing Brock could do, then she'd do it too. For his sake if not her own. She cleared her throat, pushing Yara out of her mind. They had a case to solve, and it was time for them both to knuckle down.

"Alright. Let me relay everything that Jonathan told me…"

CHAPTER FOUR

The neighborhood in Melrose was stunningly beautiful. As the sun came up over the town, Olivia watched the houses go by, three-story masterpieces lined by neat rows of perfectly manicured hedges and golden gates guarding the fronts of them. She often found her work taking her to rich communities, oddly. Rich people killing other rich people wasn't uncommon, perhaps because they had the time for elaborate plans against their rivals, but it also wasn't uncommon for the poor to target the rich. Olivia could almost understand why. Looking around at the beauty of the neighborhood, she was mentally picking out things she'd love to have for herself. She couldn't picture a life without having to work, without needing to think about money, but she imagined that it was paradise. Obviously, she would never dream of actually taking from anyone else, but she could see what drove people to do it. It was never easy to see people living the life most could only ever dream of.

But paradise was overrated.

If there were dark things lurking even in the lives of people who had the sun shining on them, then was anyone really safe?

The gated community where Kristen Burke had lived was surrounded by police cars. The gates were open now, so Olivia and Brock drove toward it. After an officer briefly stopped them to confirm their identities, they were allowed through to begin their investigation. Olivia took in the beautiful white mansion, examining the security system briefly from the outside. There was nothing subtle about the setup——Kristen was letting the world know that she was watching their every move. Cameras were placed on each corner of the house, and there was another above the front door. There was a second gate on the driveway that required a separate code from the gate to the community. Olivia wouldn't have been shocked if there were bullet proof shutters on the windows and a survivalist bunker in the backyard. How did someone ever get into a house like this one unnoticed? It would be easier trying to break into a high security prison. The family had clearly spared no expense, putting their safety as the highest priority. And yet in the end, it hadn't been enough to stop Kristen from being killed.

Olivia wondered what the woman had done to make someone go to the lengths to get inside and kill her. Not that she was blaming the victim, but she had to wonder about the motive. There were easier targets if the killer was simply out for blood or expensive things. To choose a difficult target like Kristen meant several things could be true. One, that Kristen had enemies. Or two, that the killer was willing to take on a harder task in order to show off. The third possibility was that the killer was trying to send a message of some sort. What that might be, Olivia wasn't sure. She would need more information before she could begin to speculate.

THE **HOUSEWIFE**

Olivia and Brock stepped inside the house and the first thing Olivia noticed was the lingering smell of burning. Jonathan had mentioned that Kristen had been cooking something when she had been killed. She let her nose guide her toward the smell, right toward the kitchen.

The body had been removed, but pools of blood still lay around the kitchen where Kristen had fallen. Mixed in with the blood was a mess of crumbled and broken sugar cookies, along with the metal cooking sheet that had now burned a slight scar into the tile floor. The room was clean and tidy aside from the obvious mess left by the murder. The perfection of the place had been tarnished by the horrors that had occurred. A picture-perfect life smeared with blood.

Olivia motioned for one of the officers, who brought over the crime scene photos of the scene as it had been found. She looked at them and felt her heart sinking. It was far from the first time she'd seen a dead body, of course, but that didn't make it any easier to bear. She reviewed the photos closely, trying to get any details, but knew she'd need to follow up with the morgue later anyway.

In the photos, Kristen's body lay splayed out, her eyes frozen open wide in terror and her mouth locked forever in a silent scream. She had been a beautiful woman, her hair still in perfect ringlets around her face. Her skin on her face was clear and clean, the skin of a woman who didn't have a worry in the world. But her body was riddled with stab wounds, staining her once-pristine white apron. She had been killed quickly and violently.

It almost seemed personal.

That answered at least one question for Olivia. This killer chose her for a reason. She just needed to figure out what that reason was. There were plenty of motivators——money, status, love, hate. Kristen seemed like the kind of woman who didn't make room for negativity in her life, able to throw money at her issues until they went away. But a persistent presence in her life—a person who felt strongly toward her, one way or another—might not be swayed by dollars and promises.

She passed the photos to Brock. "I'll go take a look around."

"I'll talk to the officers here," he replied.

With a nod, she stepped to inspect the rest of the house, pulling on a pair of nitrile gloves from her pocket. The kitchen had several entrances, from the dining room, the backyard and the hallway. Olivia theorized that the killer would have to have come from the backyard. If Kristen had been working on the counter—mixing bowls and flour were still set out on it—she would've seen someone coming from either of the other two entrances. She quickly clocked the earbud in Kristen's ear. The other had fallen off when she went down, and was lying in a pool of blood. If she'd been wearing both at the time she was killed, she likely wouldn't have heard someone sneaking up on her. It might've been the thing that sealed her fate.

"Initial thoughts?" Brock asked Olivia. She chewed her lips.

"The killer must have come in through the back. Unless they were already in the house, somehow. I guess that's possible, if there was a window of opportunity for them to get in while Kristen was occupied. But what I can't understand is how they got through all the security without triggering an alarm or being spotted," Olivia said. "I mean, it's difficult enough getting through the front gate in the first place. I suspect whoever made it this far must've known how to get around all of the security... or they were a friend of someone in the community and had the codes. It wouldn't have been easy to get this far though... and then to get away without being noticed?"

"And then what's the motive? We're looking at someone who killed a rich housewife in the middle of the day and then stole a bunch of her stuff. That doesn't sound like someone who has friends in the community. Rich people have rich friends, right? So why the stealing? It's not like anyone on this street is going to be short of designer handbags... or the money to buy their own. It's certainly not worth killing for."

"Trophies, perhaps? Or to throw us off the scent? The killer is obviously smart enough to evade some of the most advanced security systems in the world... anyone capable of that might already be looking to deliberately muddy the waters a bit for the investigation."

"Maybe," Brock said, though he didn't sound entirely convinced. "Still leaves us with the question of the motive, then."

"Well, perhaps the ease of the target. Not in the sense of her home security, that's for sure, but many people target women, assuming they're easier to attack. She… didn't look like she could put up much of a fight, bless her. And then there's the fact that she was a stay-at-home mom. She was likely to be home in the middle of the day. An unusual time to strike, making it more unexpected… Maybe that tells us something. Vulnerable women are so often the target of male killers…"

"Eh, I don't know. How vulnerable would she really be in this house? And why her, of anyone else on the street? If opportunity and money was the motive, why bother fiddling with the security system when you could just move on to the next house on the block? The security system is like a suit of armor."

"Not if it's disabled," Olivia reminded him. "Every armor has its chinks. So our question is, how did he get in? Weak spots or not, this whole place is decked out to stop this exact thing from happening. It would take some considerable planning and technical knowledge."

"They must've been tailing the victim for a long while before they attempted this. Either they were a part of her life and they knew when to strike, or they followed her around closely enough to guess. They knew exactly when she would be alone without her husband, and they knew how to get in unnoticed."

"Which would mean she was being targeted somehow," Brock said.

Olivia nodded. "That's what it's looking like. I don't know what to make of it… I suppose we need to take a crack at the security system ourselves."

"Well, it's a place to start. And then we're going to need an inventory of everything that's been taken. I guess that'll give us some idea of what the killer values."

Anything other than a young woman's life, Olivia thought. The young woman lying on the floor had been a wife, a mother, a friend, a daughter. And now she was reduced to a dead body.

Another corpse in the masses with a story people would forget. The killer had stolen more than her expensive things from her.

And she didn't believe that the killer was doing this for money. Sure, they'd stolen from her, but nothing significant enough to feel like this was a break-in gone wrong. A body full of stab wounds seemed like a crime of passion to her. What would possess a person to stab someone so many times? Perhaps inexperience and a fear that she would live to tell someone what had happened if they weren't thorough. But a stabbing so violent was messy and bloody. The killer would be coated head to toe in it, most likely. So how did they then get away unnoticed? Someone inexperienced with killing wasn't likely to walk away so easily.

She mulled it over in her mind while they took a look at the security logs of the house. As suspected, it had been tampered with. The morning of the murder, shortly after Kristen's husband's car had left the garage on his way to work, all of the security had blinked out. The cameras were off, the motion sensors were disabled, the alarms inside the home were not working. There was no sign that Kristen had done it herself, or that there was someone else in the house messing around with the systems. It just blacked out and never came back on. Olivia frowned as she took it all in. How had someone managed to tamper with it unless they were already in the house? But they saw no signs of anything suspicious on the rest of the footage prior to the outage. It was a mystery with no visible solutions.

"Definitely premeditated," Brock said. "We'll have to send this stuff to the lab to see if they can find anything, but I'm not holding my breath. They managed to get in here and do their job without a digital—or physical—footprint of any kind. It's flawless, really. And whoever they were, they knew how to get through the front gate too. There's no sign that anyone entered without the correct code, and the systems didn't go down like they did here. It's all so calculated."

"So someone who has been here before, and someone who knows the security systems at the house. Which implies that it was someone close to the family," Olivia said. "So what are we looking for? A scorned lover, maybe? A mistress of the husband, even? Whoever did it really wanted her to hurt, to suffer. No one stabs someone that brutally if they're looking to provide a painless death. It seems like an angry response."

"Or the husband himself."

Olivia raised an eyebrow. "Oh?"

"I mean, who would know the security system better than anyone? Who has access to the community because he lives here already?"

She considered it. "It is very often the husband, in cases like this. But then why steal the stuff?"

"Like you said. To throw us off the scent," Brock offered. "To make it look like there was a break-in. And on Valentine's Day of all days... I don't think we can discount him. It could easily be sending a message. Killing your wife on the day of love is a pretty strong one to give."

"Didn't the police say he has an alibi? He was at work all day."

"He could've done it when he came home and then just called the police. It depends on the timeline. We need to know more specifics."

"Pretty brutal, but I suppose you're right. We can't discount anything. We'll interview him and see if we can catch any inconsistencies. But if it was him, something tells me he'll have his story nailed down pretty tight."

"When has that ever stopped us from catching a killer before?" Brock said with a smile. Olivia returned one to him. She could already tell this one was going to be a doozy, but it was something to sink their teeth into. It was exactly the kind of distraction that they needed from their own issues, and there was plenty to get their brains ticking. Olivia was determined that the young woman's death wouldn't be left as a mystery.

It was time to get to work.

CHAPTER FIVE

It was several hours later when Olivia managed to gather all of Kristen Burke's family together for an interview in Kristen's living room. Thankfully, the harrowing pool of blood in the kitchen was finally being taken away and cleaned by the crime scene investigators. Olivia was interested to see what else they might find in their investigations, given that this seemed like a very well-planned murder, but for now, her focus was on creating a map of Kristen's social life, getting to know the people who knew her best. She had found that often, talking to people was just as useful as finding fingerprints and analyzing data. People tended to give all sorts of evidence away without even meaning to. And if Kristen's killer was someone

THE **HOUSEWIFE**

close to her, someone she knew, then Olivia wanted to look them in the eye and figure out what made them tick.

First on her list of suspects was the husband, but she also discovered after some digging that Kristen had quite a large family—her parents were still around, and she had two sisters. The family lived close by, but the news had only just made it to them, and Olivia had been told that they hadn't taken it well. Olivia wondered why Kristen's husband had neglected to mention what had happened to her family. That in itself was of interest to Olivia.

Now, the four members of Kristen's family had all traveled to speak to Olivia and Brock, to share their thoughts on what had gone on. The husband, Brandon, was also waiting around to give his testimony. Olivia was hoping that getting all of the people closest to Kristen in one room would prove useful to their investigation, and maybe help them shed some light on what had happened. But though the room was full of solemn, mournful faces, she made a conscious decision not to trust any of them. Often, those closest to the victims were the ones who sent them to their graves.

Olivia had opted to gather them all in the living room of Kristen's home. It was immediately obvious to Olivia that there was tension between the husband, Brandon, and the remainder of Kristen's family. The matriarch of the family, Rebecca Grace, sat tight lipped while Brandon rocked his baby in his arms. Rebecca's hair was pure silver, like even her updo was expensive, and she wore an expensive looking black mourning suit. She had clearly made an effort to dress smartly for the occasion, despite having only just heard the news. Fashion came first for her, Olivia presumed. On either side of her sat her other two daughters, Annie and Caroline, quietly dabbing at their eyes with tissues. They had the same poise as Rebecca; backs straight, dressed well, crying so soft it was almost practiced. There was a family resemblance in the younger women that linked them all together, though the main difference that Olivia noticed was that their mother's face remained stoic and untouched by tears.

Meanwhile, Kristen's father, Bruce, refused to sit down, pacing in front of the fireplace while he waited for Olivia and

Brock to begin the interview. He was a large, imposing man, but something told Olivia that he was not the one running the show in their family. All eyes drew to Rebecca, like a magnetic force.

Kristen's family seemed wary of Brandon, occasionally glancing in his direction, but never speaking to him directly, and certainly not offering him any kindness. Olivia immediately flagged that as odd. He was a part of their family, the husband of their daughter and father of their only grandson, and yet they were treating him like he was an untrustworthy stranger. Perhaps that was the reason he had neglected to get in touch with them about Kristen's death—it seemed he might be used to their cold indifference toward him. Olivia was curious to dig up the reasons for their obvious disdain, to see if there was a good reason for it. Regardless of their attitude, Brandon kept his head bowed, his eyes glistening, but his focus solely on his child, who was thankfully asleep in his arms.

Olivia cleared her throat for the room. She would learn more when they started talking.

"Thank you all for coming here to speak with us. We know this is a very difficult time for you all, but we are hoping that anything you can tell us might help us get to the bottom of what happened to Kristen. No detail is too small or unimportant, and please, feel free to speak your mind. We'll need every possible resource we can get and it starts with you."

She fixed her gaze first on the husband. "Brandon, perhaps we can start with you telling us what happened when you got home that day? I know you've given a report to the police, but we'd like to cover all bases here."

Brandon swallowed, his forehead creased. His cheeks were wet with tears. He certainly seemed distraught, despite any suspicions Olivia and Brock might have about him.

Or he was a good actor.

Rebecca certainly wasn't letting him off the hook either. She kept her gaze firmly on him, her bright blue eyes intense and almost accusing. Brandon didn't look in her direction, but Olivia bet that he could feel the weight of his mother-in-law's glare.

THE **HOUSEWIFE**

"I, um. I got home later than I planned," Brandon said, his voice trembling a little. "I'd promised Kristen I would make an effort to be back from work in time for our Valentine's dinner… but work wouldn't let me go. It's like that sometimes."

Rebecca quietly scoffed, but said nothing. Brandon ignored her, acting as though he hadn't heard her make a sound.

"What time exactly did you arrive back?" Brock asked Brandon.

"It was just after six… I remember because I checked my watch just before I went inside and knew that Kristen would be upset. I did try to hurry back. I knew she was cooking something special for us. I was really pushing the speed limit to get back home… Am I allowed to say that?"

"We're not interested in your driving habits, Brandon," Brock said, amusement making the corners of his mouth twitch. "Unless it's relevant to your wife?"

"I guess it's not. It didn't seem to get me home any quicker anyway… I started to feel like I'd really messed up. I wanted to make amends. But when I got home, I… Well, I knew immediately something was wrong. I could hear Callum screaming upstairs… that was the first sign. He rarely cries, especially when Kristen is around. And then I smelled burning coming from the kitchen… so of course I went there first."

"Not to your child?" Rebecca said snidely. This time Brandon turned to her, a snarl resting on his lips.

"I wanted to check the house wasn't on fire first." Brandon turned back to Olivia and Brock. "I thought maybe Kristen was upstairs trying to stop him from crying… I figured that maybe she'd forgotten about something in the oven. Sometimes she gets too busy with the baby. But the smoke alarm wasn't going off either, which was strange."

"Why?" Brock asked.

"I'm sure you noticed that we have a pretty top-of-the-line security system. The works. Door locks, automation, even smoke alarms. So much good that did," he scoffed. "It wasn't until afterward that I realized that our door alarm didn't beep when I got inside either. You normally have to input a code each time you come in through the front door. But it... well, I guess it wasn't on my mind. It only occurred to me afterwards that someone must have tampered with our home systems, trying to wipe out our security."

"You said you went to find your wife?" Olivia asked, pushing him onward with his story. Brandon's breath seemed to catch in his throat as he reached the crux of the tale.

"Well I... I rushed into the kitchen and... I found..."

Brandon trailed off, swallowing back tears. They all knew what he had found there. Olivia nodded reassuringly to him, urging him to keep going.

"What did you do then?"

"I... it took me a few minutes to move, I think. I was shell-shocked. I couldn't stop looking at her, just lying there... I've never seen a dead body before. And it was hard for me to make the connection between my wife and the woman on the floor. I think I just snapped. And when I finally came to my senses, I didn't immediately call the police. I went upstairs to check on Callum. I didn't mean to leave him alone for so long, but at the moment... I'm ashamed to admit it wasn't the first thing on my mind."

Rebecca made another noise of disapproval, but she fell quiet after a stern look from her husband. Olivia could see that her presence was irking Brandon, his eyebrows knitted together, but he still didn't attempt to butt heads with her. Olivia could see him weighing it up, but in the end, he picked his battle.

"What I meant to say is... seeing my wife there... I couldn't think straight. Of course I would normally have gone to my son first. But the circumstances were anything but normal."

"We understand," Brock said with a nod. "You're not on trial here for your reaction to your wife's death, sir. We're just looking for an honest account."

Brandon nodded. "Right. Of course. Well... when I finally came to my senses, I went downstairs to call our panic button. The security system that we installed is very complex, and we have a number of places where we can call for help. It's supposed to put us straight through to our security company and the police. But it didn't work. And that's when I realized that someone had disabled

THE **HOUSEWIFE**

the entire security system. Or that it was broken somehow... but given the fact that someone came in and killed my wife the one day it wasn't working, I assume they must have disabled it. I don't know how they did it... even I don't always remember how it works. Kristen was the one who wanted it installed and she obsessed over it, always making sure it was working. It made her feel safe, so I was in favor of it. But in her time of need... it just stopped functioning."

"And now my daughter is dead," Bruce said coldly. "I will have someone held responsible for this. The swine that sold this security system clearly scammed her. If it doesn't work then what did she fork out thousands of dollars for? Why didn't it save her life?"

"Let's not jump to conclusions, Bruce," Brandon said calmly. "Whoever did this came in with a plan. They could've disabled it themselves."

"Why are you defending some big company that took your money?" Rebecca snapped. "If they'd done their job, none of this would've happened."

"You just ignored what I said. It didn't just suddenly fail and then someone snuck in to kill her. It's too much of a coincidence. It was working that morning when I left, so I don't think it was on the fritz."

Bruce shook his head. "I always knew you were spineless, kid, but not like this. Your wife is dead and you're not even going to fight for her, huh? You're not going to show up for your wife today?"

Anger finally got the better of Brandon, flashing through his eyes. "I never said—"

"Please. Settle down," Brock said, shooting a look at Rebecca and Bruce. "We'd like to hear Brandon's account without your input. This is not the time for you to go to battle with your son-in-law."

Rebecca's mouth dropped open, clearly horrified at having someone tell her what to do, but her husband put a hand on her shoulder to keep her from retaliating. He took a steadying breath, clearly reminding himself that he wasn't the one with authority in the room. He nodded to Brock respectfully, and he turned back to Brandon to continue his questioning.

"So you called the police manually instead?"

Brandon nodded. "I was forced to. But they came as quickly as they could. While I was waiting for them to arrive, I tried to calm Callum down, walking him around the house to settle him. Kristen was always so good at keeping him calm… it was like he sensed that she was gone. I know that's not possible… but it just felt that way." Brandon sighed, holding Callum closer to his chest. "I was trying to keep my mind occupied, walking through the house. Well, anywhere but the kitchen. I wasn't about to put my son in the same room as his dead mother. So I was just sort of pacing around… and that's when I began to realize that things were missing from the house. I thought I was going crazy at first… but I kept looking around and I'd see things weren't where they were supposed to be. We had this little ornament on a coffee table in the lounge… that was gone. And I knew it was relevant because it was worth a small fortune, according to Kristen. Someone with expensive taste had swiped it. And when I went up to Kristen's closet, that's when it confirmed my suspicions of the robbery. A bunch of her designer handbags were gone, and a lot of expensive jewelry. You can see the obvious gaps in the closet where things have been taken, or else I might not have noticed. She has all these little shelves for her bags and three or four of them are now empty. It kind of winded me, realizing that someone had explored our home and just helped themselves. It began to hit me that this wasn't just a murder… whoever did this wanted to steal from Kristen. And they were willing to kill her for what she has."

Olivia chewed her lips. Something wasn't adding up to her. A violent stabbing like what Kristen had experienced was certainly performed by someone with a lot of anger inside them… but surely the motive wasn't a few designer handbags and a handful of jewelry? She knew that they held more value than she estimated, but it didn't feel like enough to drive someone to murder.

And then there was something else that struck her as strange. She had assumed the killer would be a man, based on the violence behind it and the motives they'd toyed with. But what man would

THE **HOUSEWIFE**

murder over designer handbags, ornaments and jewelry? She knew that some men were interested in those things, and yet it struck her as more likely that a woman would want them, not a man. Was she mistaken? Was the murderer a jealous woman, wanting the life Kristen had led? Or was a man doing it for his lover, taking trophies from the scene to take home to her?

She needed to know more before she could speculate. She took a deep breath and turned her attention back to Brandon.

"Is there anything else you might be able to tell us about the stolen items? And do you have any clue of who might want to do this?'

Brandon wavered. "Honestly? I don't understand any of this. Kristen is… *was*… an incredible woman. Everyone loved her. Even the staff we hired to help around the house… they all took to her. She paid them very generously, chatted to them, and made friends with many of them. She was a good person. It feels to me like anyone who knew her… *really* knew her… would never be capable of doing something like this to her."

"Why don't you tell us more about the staff you hired?" Brock asked. "They would've all had access to the house in some way, shape or form…"

Brandon shook his head. "I don't think they can possibly be related to what happened here. We have several cleaners, but they adore Kristen. The gardener is practically in love with her, even though he's fifteen years her senior… We had a few nannies come and go, but Kristen preferred to look after Callum herself, so she sent them away, but she paid them well, gave them good references… there was no bitterness there. And then there's her interior designer… a woman she's been working with for years. She's forever redecorating, and she's never once been unhappy with the work. So I don't see there being any bad blood there either. Though I never really got to spend any time with these people. I was always working…"

"The very backbone of the household, aren't you?' Rebecca said, rolling her eyes. "Stop playing the martyr, *Brandon*. You chose to work instead of being home with your wife. God knows your salary wasn't what kept you in this beautiful home. You've been living off our money all this time."

Brandon's face turned thunderous. "So which is it? That I'm living off your money or that I abandoned your daughter with our child at home to work? Nothing I've ever done has been good enough for you. Just because I never drove a fancy car and my salary paid less than the inheritance Kristen got from her rich grandfather. I wanted to work, I wanted an ordinary life. I never needed all of this. What more do you want from me?"

"You clearly married her for the money," Rebecca sneered. "I knew you were a gold digger from the moment I laid eyes on you."

"I didn't even *know* about the money until we got engaged. Are you implying that I couldn't love your daughter without millions of dollars hanging over our heads? Because honestly, at this point I wish she'd been dirt poor. Maybe then she'd still be alive!" he thundered.

The entire family sat there in shock. Olivia took the moment to scribble in her journal but made no move to stop the argument. This was all valuable information.

"It would've saved me a whole lot of trouble," Brandon went on bitterly. "I never wanted any of this. And I've never spent a single *dollar* of her money. She was quite capable of squandering it herself."

"Don't talk about Kristen that way!" Annie said tearfully. "You always made her feel so guilty for *having things*. What was wrong with her spending the money? It was *hers."*

"Don't I know it," Brandon said, glaring at Rebecca. "I've never been allowed to forget it. She was free to do what she wanted, and I resent the implication that I somehow *held her back*. You know Kristen did exactly what she wanted, *when* she wanted every day of her life. I've spent the past few years treading on eggshells, trying not to upset any of you over something stupid. And where did it get me? Now I'm alone. I'm certainly not a part of this family anymore. At least there's one silver lining of this ugly mess."

Olivia watched the argument unfold, seeing Brandon's temper rising inside him. She could understand his anger, given the treatment from Kristen's family, but there was violence in his eyes. She'd seen it so many times before in bad men, men who would willingly stab their wives repeatedly and cover it all up in the same breath. Men who would lie to her face about everything they'd done. Was Brandon that kind of man? She wasn't sure. If so, he'd gone to great lengths to throw them off the scent—the failed security system, the stolen items, the burning cookies in the oven and the abandoned child.

But wasn't that the sign of a mastermind pulling the strings?

Brandon stood up, clutching his son close to him.

"If we're done here, I'd like to leave. I need to put my son down for a nap," Brandon said, his eyes blazing.

Rebecca smirked. "That's right. You walk away from her. Wouldn't be the first time."

Brandon whirled on Rebecca, his teeth gritted. "Don't you ever—"

Callum began to cry in Brandon's arms and his face softened. He kissed his son on the top of his head, stroking his back.

"I'm sorry, kid. I'm sorry."

Brandon left the room without another word. Rebecca sat back in her seat, looking satisfied with her handiwork.

"He was trouble from the start, that one," she said coldly.

Olivia chewed her lip.

"What did you mean… *it wouldn't be the first time?*"

Rebecca sniffed. "Well, he was always flighty. The first sign of trouble and he'd go storming out on Kristen. Used to leave her in puddles of tears every time they fought. My daughter was a sweet fool. She adored that man, no matter what he did."

"It's not uncommon to walk away from an argument every now and then," Brock tried to reason. "Perhaps he feels the pressure from your side of the family, Mrs Grace. Have you considered that the pressure pushed him to boiling point?"

Rebecca scowled. "I've always had money, young man. I know how to spot leeches when they come to suck us dry. That man had a nose for it and he sniffed her out. I don't care what he claims, he was aware of her finances. And maybe walking away every so often is normal, but I swear, the one thing that kept him coming back was the money. Any man of real substance would walk away and stay gone. But he'd come crawling back on his hands and knees, begging forgiveness so that he could keep living in this house, basking in *our* money." Rebecca paused for breath, her impassioned speech leaving her chest heaving. "And of course, that money will be *his* now. I tried to get my darling daughter to sign a prenup, to take precautions, to let *us* handle her will. But of course, stubborn as she was, she insisted everything would be fine. And now she's dead."

"Rebecca… be careful of what you're implying," Bruce said gruffly. Rebecca lifted her chin up high.

"I am not *implying* anything. I'm *telling* you. That man killed my daughter for her money. Case closed." Rebecca turned to Olivia. "You can go about your fancy investigation however you like. But I can guarantee, all roads will lead you home. *He* had access to the house, *he* had access to the security system, *he* had everything to gain from her death. And *you* just let my daughter's killer walk away from you."

CHAPTER SIX

REBECCA GRACE DID NOT APPEAR TO BE THE KIND OF person who let things go.

Olivia and Brock continued their interviews with Kristen's family, but it quickly became clear that Rebecca was running the show on behalf of the family. She spoke for them all, though sometimes Bruce attempted to rein her in or to steer the conversation. She made her disdain for her son-in-law clear, making baseless accusations about him being a horrific, money-grubbing, good-for-nothing loser. Olivia had heard it all before, but there was something about Rebecca Grace that intrigued her. She was so committed to her bit that she barely stopped for breath, passionately tearing Brandon down at any opportunity she had.

"Did Kristen ever share any of your concerns about Brandon?" Brock asked Rebecca. She huffed, shaking her head.

"Well, of course not! She was a young, pretty fool in love. She just thought we were being overprotective. She didn't see the danger in it all. Nothing I said would change her mind."

"From what Brandon told us, Kristen was a bright girl. She chose the life she wanted, surely?" Olivia asked. "She knew she wanted to be a mother, to spend her time at home… and she got to do that. While Brandon was opting for a more ordinary life, going to an ordinary job, not relying on the Grace family fortune…"

"So he claims," Rebecca snorted. "He has to say that though, doesn't he? He has to pretend he's so humble so that he's not judged for going after a woman in a better position than him. How *emasculating* that would be for a man like him. More concerned with his image than anything else."

Brock shot Olivia a look, one of their quick telepathic glances. She immediately knew what it meant: he was going on the offensive. "Well, from what I could tell, he didn't seem vain to me…"

"Oh, please. He preens like a woman any chance he gets," Rebecca replied, raising her nose in the air.

"So you believe that he was keeping up appearances?" Brock asked. "That he only kept working to make it seem as though he wasn't interested in money?"

"Oh, absolutely. And it's worked, hasn't it? He's got you convinced. He's a snake in the grass. You don't know he's venomous until it's far too late," she declared. "And to think that man is going to have sole control of my grandson now. If Brandon has his way, he won't have anything to do with me or the rest of the Grace family—aside from the inheritance, of course. Assuming that he gets away with his crimes," she said, her hand gripping the arm of the couch tightly. Olivia folded her arms, watching Rebecca with interest.

"Perhaps you can be a little more specific about your concerns. Aside from marrying your daughter against your wishes, how else has Brandon given you a bad impression?"

THE **HOUSEWIFE**

Rebecca considered the question, her lips pursed. "Well, I know his kind. His whole family is exactly the same. They never got anywhere in life alone so they piggybacked off their betters. You think he's the first one to try this trick? I had my fair share of admirers back in the day, but there was no chance I'd lower myself to be with just anybody. I married for love to a man I could trust... it makes sense to keep circles tight, to stop leeches from begging their way in. The way Brandon did. I mean, it's no coincidence that Brandon's sister ended up marrying one of Kristen's old school friends."

"You don't think it's possible that they met through Kristen and Brandon and just happened to like one another? That they hit it off?" Brock said, the corners of his mouth twitching. Olivia could tell that he thought Rebecca was ridiculous, and to some extent, Olivia agreed. But she seemed so sure in her opinion of Brandon that she was sure that if they dug deep enough, they'd find something more to her hatred.

"I think it was entirely planned. Do you know what the chances are of falling in love that way? Meeting someone so coincidentally? Next to none."

"Do you have evidence to back that up? A graph, maybe?" Brock asked tiredly. Olivia had to hide a smile as Rebecca glared at him.

"Don't brush me off so easily. This is my world, not yours... that much is clear. I don't need to explain myself. They both married rich to lift themselves up. And now, don't be shocked when his sister bumps off her husband for his money too..."

"Brandon claimed he had no idea about the money before they married."

Rebecca scoffed. "Of course he did. Kristen used to swear blind that she kept her money quiet, that he always paid for their dates, that she only ever stayed at his place to avoid him finding out... but I'm sure it's a lie. Her head was in the clouds half the time. I don't think it would occur to her to be so careful. Look, you asked for my opinion and I'm giving it to you. I've known him a lot longer than you have and I just don't trust him, okay? Never have and never will."

"Your concern is noted, but I'm afraid that's not enough for us to pin this on him, Mrs Grace," Brock said. "But we will find whoever did this. I promise it. If it's him, we'll soon know."

"Then you'd better start by digging up some dirt on that family of his. And take a closer look at him, too. Try and find out what's keeping him from being at home, because it sure as hell isn't work. Out every night, always coming up with some excuse to be away from his wife... since he married her, it's like he's given up on her, like he's already got what he needed. Why else would Kristen be on the phone to me crying all the time? She was neglected."

"Marriages are complicated. I'm sure we can attest to that," Bruce said with a sigh. "You always did keep a collar on her, Rebecca. You made her sensitive and paranoid. Convinced her that everyone was out to get her."

"It was better that way. At least no one could ever take her for a ride," Rebecca sniffed. "He's up to something, I'm sure of it. Or else what would be keeping him away from his son all day every day?" Rebecca sighed, rising from her seat. "But this is your issue now. Nothing will bring back my daughter, and I am in mourning. Since you won't take me seriously, then I suppose I better hope you're good at the other parts of your job. I'm done here."

Rebecca swanned out of the room, quickly followed by her two daughters. Bruce left last, pausing to shake Brock's hand, but not Olivia's.

"Good luck," he said before leaving the room. Brock clenched his jaw.

"Did you see that?"

"What?"

"Well, of course you did. He just avoided shaking your hand! I can't believe he just dismissed you like that. That was so rude and old-fashioned. I should go after him..."

Olivia put a hand on his chest to stop him. "He's... traditional. They all are. They have that old money vibe to them, and they're protective of their way of life. He probably doesn't think a woman should be in this job."

"Then he should be educated. You're one of the best in the game. I want to say something to him... it's wrong."

Olivia smiled. "So are plenty of things. But I think we can let go of the fact that he didn't shake my hand, can't we? We've got other things to worry about."

Brock's brow creased and he looked as though he might argue, but after a moment, he let out a breath.

"Fine. But if he does that again, I'm saying something. I won't have you being disrespected like that."

Olivia nodded, lowering her head a little to hide her smile. She definitely didn't need Brock to fight her battles for her, but sometimes it was nice that he tried. His protectiveness hadn't gone unnoticed. She knew he'd do anything to cover her back, the way she would for him too. It made her feel better, knowing that he was on her side through thick and thin. It was what made them such a good team.

"Come on. We've got things to do. Let's see if we can learn a little more about Brandon Burke."

⁓

There was no record cleaner than Brandon Burke's.

Olivia and Brock spent the rest of their day doing a deep dive on Brandon and his family. While Brandon mourned in his mansion with his son, they investigated his online presence, his job at the local bank branch and his legal documents. Rebecca had been right about one thing—Brandon was the sole benefactor in Kristen's will. Considering Kristen's wealth, that had to be something they looked into. He had the means to take everything from her, and the will gave him a motive. However, they also noted that the will had been created after their wedding and before the birth of their child.

"So this will is nothing new," Olivia said as they searched through the document. "It might not count Callum in, but he wasn't in the picture back then... and I guess Kristen hadn't seen any reason to change it. Why would she? It's not like the rest of her family would need the money if she passed away. It makes sense that it would all go to her immediate family. Besides, Callum is *their* son. It's not as if Brandon has any intentions of taking the money away from his child… right?"

"One would hope," Brock said. "Which raises the question… if the will was always going to include Brandon, if he was always in line for the money, then why would he kill her now? Did he find some immediate need for the money? Perhaps he ran into some debt?"

"Not according to his bank statements… the ones he quite willingly handed over, we should remember," Olivia said. "The way Rebecca tells it, he hasn't got a dollar to his name, but this tells another story. He's got a good credit score, he keeps on top of his credit cards, his Christmas bonus was substantial and he's been saving for donkey's years."

"It's almost like he's familiar with banking and money management…"

"Well, exactly! He's got a decent job and he looks after his money. He barely spends a penny outside of bills and contributions to the house. He's set up a college fund for Callum in his name, which he certainly doesn't need to. Kristen could've sent him to college without blinking an eye. So where did all this mistrust come from on Rebecca's part? He's doing fine, and if he walked away from this marriage, he wouldn't exactly be strapped for cash. So is he still a potential suspect, realistically? He didn't seem like a man with something to hide, did he?"

"I guess not. But Rebecca did seem very suspicious of him."

"I don't imagine there are many people Rebecca Grace isn't suspicious of. She thinks everyone is out to get her and her money. I don't imagine she would've been satisfied with Kristen marrying anyone less than a billionaire. Not even a millionaire would have been enough."

Brock chuckled. "Now maybe we're being harsh. But you're right. We can't base everything off Rebecca's thoughts. She's not the most trustworthy source. We're going to need to dig a bit deeper if we're going to find something here. So he's not in financial trouble. Maybe we should look at where he's spending his money. Rebecca made claims that he's always out, that he's

THE HOUSEWIFE

rarely home for his wife and kid. Even Brandon said it himself that he was home late a lot."

"He said it was for work… and his spending habits look pretty clean to me."

"He works for a bank. Is there really any reason for him to be home late? The more I think about it, the more suspicious it seems to me. He knew that dinner with his wife was important, on Valentine's Day, and he still couldn't get home before six? I don't know… is that his way of buying him the amount of time he needed to kill her?"

"I don't know, Brock… it still doesn't add up. What about all the things that were stolen? Are you really implying he stole from himself? What would be the point in that?"

"I'm just saying, it's a place to start. I mean, look at this from the day of the murder. He paid a pretty hefty sum for his lunch if it was just him. He had time to go out for lunch but he couldn't make it back to his wife on time? On *Valentine's Day?* What if this restaurant isn't even in town?"

"Okay, I guess that is a little strange. But the payment was made at two in the afternoon. That's four hours before he claimed to get home. It could mean nothing."

"Or it could mean everything," Brock countered. "He didn't think to mention it to us, did he? After such a thorough rundown of his day, he forgets to mention the expensive lunch he went out for? I want to talk to him again, see if his story lines up. That's okay with you?"

"Well, I won't say no to that. Let's hope he isn't keeping things from us."

CHAPTER SEVEN

"Sorry to keep you, Brandon. I know this is a tough time right now. We just wanted to ask a few follow-up questions and make sense of your timeline. Is that okay with you?"

"Of course. I'm not sure what else I could even do right now anyway. I want to help," Brandon said as he sat down on the sofa opposite Olivia and Brock. He'd laid Callum down for a nap, but he kept a baby monitor close to him. He looked tired, Olivia noticed. She wasn't surprised. He'd become a single parent overnight. That was bound to take a toll.

But now, it was time to figure out if that was deliberate on his part.

THE **HOUSEWIFE**

"We noticed on your receipts that you actually went out for lunch several hours before you found your wife dead. You paid your bill at four minutes past two," Olivia said. "We looked up the restaurant, and it's not in town. Since we thought you were at work yesterday, we have to ask about it…"

Brandon smacked his forehead with the palm of his hand. "Crap. I'm sorry, I should have mentioned. I was working, but out of town. I sometimes travel during the week. There was a conference that a few of us were sent to on behalf of the bank… all pretty boring stuff, no one wanted to go considering it was Valentine's Day. We all had places to be. But they give you a long lunch before the debrief at the end of the day. I guess it's to make it feel like it was worth going all of that way for such a useless conference… I went out with a few pals for food and then returned to the conference. I'm sorry, I guess I forgot that the police need me to be pretty specific."

Olivia caught Brock's eye out of the corner of her own. They were prepared for him to spin a story like this. They had looked up the restaurant themselves; Daphne's Bistro was no dive diner or casual lunch spot. It had glowing reviews online, and four dollar signs on the engine search to indicate that it was expensive. Olivia very much doubted that Brandon, a man who seemed concerned with money and not overspending, was taking all of his pals to an expensive bistro for a work lunch. She wished she could see the receipt in detail. She was willing to bet pretty much anything that the food ordered was for two, not for a group. But who had he met for lunch, and why was he trying to hide it from them?

If he was lying to them about this, what else was he lying about?

Olivia shifted in her seat. She didn't want to give away that they were on to him. She'd seen this scenario before—people always thought they were smart enough to cover their tracks by claiming to have 'forgotten' important details. They relied far too heavily on human error, and that was a rookie mistake on Brandon's part. Now that they knew he was a liar, it would be much easier to see through his act.

"So it's a bit of a drive back home from the restaurant… an hour and a half, and hour forty, maybe."

"It took me longer, the traffic was pretty bad. I left the conference at ten past four. Took me forever to get out of the parking lot because some idiot held up traffic," Brandon said smoothly. Olivia searched his face for signs that he was lying, but he kept his expression level. He was good. A seasoned liar, perhaps. Had he been hiding something from Kristen all along? Had she started to suspect something was up? Was that what had gotten her killed?

"To make it home for just after six, correct?"

"Yes, that's right."

"Is there any chance we can back this up with anyone?" Olivia asked. "Your car is pretty fancy. Does it have a GPS tracker so that we can follow your location? A routine check, of course. Just to definitively rule you out."

Brandon shrugged. "Sure. But my car only went to the conference center. One of my friends drove us to lunch. I'm sure you'll find that it all adds up."

Olivia chewed the inside of her cheek. That was interesting. Was Brandon so aware of his virtual footprint that he had someone else pick him up and drive him around? Did he deliberately opt not to drive his car to anywhere suspicious? It was smart, really. It gave him some leeway with his alibi. Perhaps she was being overly suspicious of him—they still had no proof that he was up to anything, much less that he was the killer. But the more Olivia uncovered, the more she felt like Brandon had something to hide.

"Well, we still need to take a look if that's okay with you? It's standard procedure, we have to try and back up everyone's alibis in any way we can," Brock said. Brandon shrugged again.

"Do what you've gotta do. Please, ask anything of me. Nothing is too much. Not when you're going to find out who did this to my wife."

Yes we are, Olivia thought. Brandon handed Brock the keys to his car and Brock went out to take a look at the dashboard while Olivia continued her questioning. Olivia smiled at him, not wanting him to know that she didn't trust him.

THE **HOUSEWIFE**

"While we're here… I just wanted to discuss your wife's family a little. What's the deal with them? They seem very harsh on you. And there's some tension there, if you don't mind me saying so."

Brandon scoffed, raising an eyebrow. "Yeah, I guess you could say that. Look, I get it. There are a lot of gold diggers out there. It would be easy for them to distrust a guy like me… I came from nothing. But I worked hard to get where I am—and I didn't want to put that to waste just because I married someone rich. I mean, if we were to ever break up, I wanted money of my own. I had no intention of trying to take money from Kristen in a divorce settlement if it ever happened."

"So you prepared for the worst?"

Brandon straightened up a little. "I guess you could say that. But when you grow up poor, that tends to be the default. I wasn't about to put myself in trouble by not keeping some money aside for emergencies. Like I said, I never spent Kristen's money. It made me uncomfortable, all that money… and the thing is, I'm kind of proud. If you think Rebecca's disapproving of my arrangement with Kristen, you should hear my mother's thoughts on it. She thinks that Kristen saw me as a charity case. Which is why I decided never to touch her money. I wanted to prove that if things had been different, if Kristen and I had never met, I would've been fine alone. If anything, I'd be better off money wise. I pay thirty percent of the bills, and running a home like this one isn't cheap. If we lived somewhere else, I wouldn't have that hanging over my head. You see, this goes through my mind a lot. I can't win in the eyes of our families—either way, I'm a scrounger, a social climber, whatever they want to call me. But I know that's not true."

Olivia thought about what Rebecca had said about Brandon, claiming he was vain. She now saw what she meant, in a way—Brandon was concerned about what people thought of him, but in the sense that he wanted to seem independent. Where Rebecca saw a deceitful thief, Brandon looked in the mirror and saw an honest, hardworking man.

And he was still keen to uphold his image. He barely stopped for breath, trying to build his case up further.

"I make good money at my job and I've never relied on anyone else... including my wife. Rebecca was so sure that I wanted Kristen's money, but I never touched a penny of it. I paid for my car myself. Any pricey possessions I have are bought with my money, unless they were gifts from Kristen, but I'm pretty minimalist anyway. Kristen could've told you that much. Yes, okay, she bought the house, but that was because she refused to live in my apartment. We could've afforded somewhere in between, but she was used to a certain way of living. So she bought the house outright. It's all in her name, not mine. I'm basically a renter here, paying a percentage of the mortgage like I told you before."

"And now that will go to you, from the will."

"I guess it will."

"And that's put Rebecca on edge. Given the circumstances."

Brandon sighed. "Yeah, well I can understand how it looks. Anything looks bad on a guy when you've already decided you don't like him. And everyone has money on their minds in some way. It makes the world go around, how can we not consider it? But I had nothing to gain from her death. I love her. I... I was devastated when I came home and saw what had happened. After all our precautions... it all just feels so pointless. I don't know why anyone would think I wanted this. If anything, this complicates everything so much more... how am I supposed to work when I'll be raising a child alone? How am I supposed to live in this house after what happened here? I just want to get out. I don't think I can bear any of it. The life I thought I would have... well, it's over now."

Olivia nodded in understanding. He was saying all the right things. He was making sense. But until his backstory checked out, she wouldn't be satisfied. She wanted to believe that he wouldn't kill his wife, that he had nothing to do with it. But right now, he was the only person they had with a motive to kill. He had so much to gain, if you believed he was interested in Kristen's money. Olivia wasn't convinced that he was, but she had to follow the lead to the end.

Brock returned from the car, tossing Brandon the car keys. Olivia looked up at him expectantly and Brock shrugged.

THE **HOUSEWIFE**

"Car GPS checks out," Brock said. "The car went to the conference center and then straight back. The journey took around two hours, as Brandon told us."

Olivia forced a smile for Brandon. "Well then, looks like we got what we came for."

"Great," Brandon said with a tight smile. "You can call on me if you need me, any time. But I won't be here if you come calling. I don't want to get in the way of the police, so I'll be staying at the hotel I've been at until we get all this stuff sorted out. And you've got my number."

"Of course. Thank you for your time," Olivia said.

Brock and Olivia returned to their car and Olivia sighed into the seat. She glanced at Brock.

"Any thoughts?"

"Well, he's definitely lying about something," he said. "My best guess is that he did something that day that he doesn't want us to know about. And given that his wife died sometime between him having that lunch and him supposedly arriving home... we need to follow up further. Maybe we can call his work and see what they have to say about it? I mean, he was at the conference center, that much is true. What about these buddies he supposedly had lunch with? Someone drove him to the restaurant, or he called a car."

"I don't want to ask his co-workers until it's necessary. If Brandon thinks we're sniffing around him too much, he might block our way. This money he's coming into will change everything for him. He's got the money for the best lawyers in town, and I don't want that getting in our path. I say we should go to the restaurant first, while Brandon is still cocky thinking we bought his story. Maybe we can speak to the staff and find out who he was there with. If he's lied, then we can pull him up on it again. And if he was meeting with someone to plan the murder of his wife, then we'll have information on whoever he was there with."

"Alright, that sounds like a plan. And hey, this place looks pretty nice. Maybe we could stop for a bite to eat..."

"Is there ever a time you're not thinking about your next meal?"

Brock cocked his head to the side. "While I'm eating? Actually, that's a lie. I was daydreaming about dinner this morning at breakfast…"

⁂

One thing did check out in Brandon's story—the drive to the restaurant was blocked by miles of traffic. It took almost two and a half hours for Olivia and Brock to drive to Daphne's Bistro, and by the time they got there, even Olivia was considering trying to snag a reservation. It had been a long day, and hunger gnawed at her stomach. Still, they weren't there to eat. They had some lies to unravel.

But getting into the restaurant to speak to someone was easier said than done. They had to spend another twenty minutes finding somewhere to park nearby and then they waited in line for what felt like an eternity just to speak to the host. Brock puffed out a sigh.

"Can you smell that? Right now, someone is about to tuck into a nice, juicy porterhouse… and I'm very aware of the fact that it isn't me."

Olivia rolled her eyes. "If you get through this next part without mentioning food, I'll let you pick somewhere for us to get dinner. But we sure as hell can't afford this place."

"How do you know? There's no prices on the menu… "

"Exactly."

Finally, they reached the front of the line. The host, a sweet blonde girl, greeted them with a pleasant smile.

"Thank you for waiting. I'm afraid that the wait for a table for two is still pretty long without a reservation… with it being the week of Valentine's and all… "

"Actually, we're not here for food. Though we wish we were," Brock said. He pulled out a picture of Brandon on his phone. "We're in the middle of an investigation with the FBI. This man dined

THE **HOUSEWIFE**

here on Valentine's Day, but we are looking into who attended the dinner with him. Would you happen to recognize him?"

She frowned. "Um. Sorry. I didn't work that day, but the other girls were on the floor."

"Can you grab them for us?" Olivia asked.

She looked over to the floor and then back to them. "Um. It's pretty hectic in there right now…"

Olivia didn't want to have to call a manager or escalate this any further than she absolutely had to. "Look, we just need to talk to whoever served this man. It'll just take a minute. It's for a murder investigation."

The girl's mouth dropped open, her bright painted lips falling into a perfect O. "Oh, well, um. Okay. Um. I'll go around and ask. Can you…"

"Just take my phone with you," Brock offered, placing it into her hand. "Don't go snooping around in there, though…"

The host gave him a nervous laugh before she excused herself to zip between the tables, bouncing around the servers as they navigated the crowded restaurant. Olivia and Brock stood to one side and waited. A few minutes later, the host returned with an older woman, dressed smartly for work with her auburn hair as neat as a pin. She offered a bright smile to Olivia and Brock.

"Hi there. I was this man's server on Valentine's Day… is there anything I can help you with?"

"Yes, we need to know a few things about the meal he had here," Olivia had.

"Well I can assure you he had excellent service," the woman beamed with a light laugh. Then she cleared her throat. "Sorry, I'm in service industry mode. How can I help?"

"We need to know who he dined with, if you can remember," Brock said.

"I do remember. He was here with his wife. I remember because they seemed very loved up, it was kind of sweet. Valentine's day can be a bit sickly sweet, but they were a lovely couple."

Olivia glanced at Brock. That certainly didn't add up. Not when Kristen was at home with their baby. Not when it was highly likely that Kristen was killed during the time Brandon was out for lunch.

"Can you describe the woman he was with?" Olivia asked, her heart hammering against her chest. The woman frowned.

"I mean, sure. She was very beautiful… dark skinned, this gorgeous afro hair… She was tall, very slim. She didn't eat much of her salad. Shame on her. It costs an arm and a leg to eat here."

Olivia blinked, but didn't let her surprise show too much. She called up a photo of Kristen from her phone and asked. "So he wasn't with this woman?"

The server inspected the image and frowned. "Nope. Sorry."

"Alright. Thank you. That's all we needed to know."

"Sure." She glided back to her table and immediately pasted on her service industry face.

"Well, that's certainly not Kristen," Brock said with a whistle once they stepped out of the restaurant.

"It certainly isn't."

Olivia let out a breath. They now knew that Brandon had absolutely been lying to them. But what did it mean? He was cheating on his wife, that much was certain. But what wasn't certain was what that meant for Kristen.

Had he killed her for love?

CHAPTER EIGHT

"You don't think this can wait until the morning?" Brock asked as they drove straight for the hotel where Brandon was staying with his son. Brock had a burger in his hand from the drive through and he was eating it as he drove. It was all they'd had the time for when Olivia had insisted that it was vital that they went to speak with Brandon right away.

"No, I don't think it can wait, Brock. Brandon has been lying through his teeth to us ever since we met. How are we supposed to trust him when he can't seem to get his story straight? And now, he's got a second motive."

"Which is?"

"Bump off his wife so that he and his mystery lover can have the house and the money, obviously."

"Olivia, you said it yourself, the guy doesn't care about money. If he did, then all he needed to do was be present in his marriage and enjoy the life of luxury…"

"Yes, but this complicates things, right? He might not care much about the money, but I'll bet his lover does, given her choice of restaurant for their date. And now so much of this feels like it could make sense… the expensive jewelry and handbags going missing? Maybe they were tokens for his lover, to show her what he's willing to do for her. It just so happens that it was a good way of throwing us off the scent too. God, if this really is him, then he's good. But not good enough, clearly."

Olivia's heart was racing like she was in the middle of a car chase. It was so early in their investigation, and yet it felt like they might already have their man. Was it possible that they'd struck lucky already? It was almost too good to be true.

But that didn't mean it wasn't.

Olivia texted Brandon ahead of their arrival to let him know that they were coming to see him. She didn't say what the purpose of the visit was, not wanting him to run scared—and if he did, she'd know they had him cornered. She was sure he wouldn't suspect their reason for wanting to speak to him. He texted back to let them know he'd meet them in the lobby. It was getting close to midnight now, and Olivia was surprised that he was still awake.

"Maybe the guilt is keeping him up," Olivia muttered out loud. Brock chuckled.

"Or a screaming newborn."

"You don't think he did it, do you?"

"I don't know what I think," he said diplomatically. "I know he's got the motive and the means… I mean, he could've easily been the one to shut down the security system after he left for work, and this secret lover storyline certainly puts him in a bad light, especially with all the money involved in Kristen's death."

"Not to mention that Rebecca was hugely suspicious of him…"

THE HOUSEWIFE

"Yeah, you're right. There's a lot of things adding up. But the simplest answer isn't always the right one. It would make a lot of sense for him to be the killer... and yet I still feel like we might be missing something. Sometimes an affair is just an affair. How many times have we blamed a scorned lover only to be wrong? This could be the same again. He might have his reasons for his behavior."

"I guess we'll find out."

The hotel parking lot was pretty quiet with just a few cars scattered around. Melrose was a very wealthy town, but it wasn't exactly a tourist hotspot, so the almost deserted hotel wasn't out of place. It was, however, a little creepy. There were no lights in the parking lot, and Olivia fought the urge to use the flashlight on her phone. It felt like there was someone creeping around in the shadows, only one step behind them at all times.

But when Olivia approached the hotel and heard the thin wail of a baby crying, she knew that Brandon was waiting for them there. As they entered, they saw Brandon sitting on the sofa in front of the main desk, cradling Callum desperately. He looked exhausted now, and on the edge of tears. Olivia and Brock exchanged a glance. They were looking at a broken man.

But not necessarily an innocent one.

"Hey," Brandon said wearily. "I'll take you up to the room. I think Callum's crying is driving the front desk crazy. Possibly me too... I just can't seem to get him to quiet down."

Brandon led them to the elevator and as they took it up to the third floor, Callum's cries ricocheted off the tinny walls. Olivia winced. The poor kid had no idea just how hard his life had become, but he was certainly crying like he understood. Olivia didn't want to imagine how much worse things would get for Callum if they found out that Brandon killed Kristen. She wondered what would be worse—a life in the foster system or a life under the thumb of his grandmother.

Brandon let out a sigh of relief as they made it to his room. He nudged the door open with his hip. He hadn't even bothered to lock it. He sat down on the edge of the bed, rocking Callum back and forth, his large hands making his child look even smaller. It made Olivia a little nervous. How were they supposed to question Brandon about a murder when he had such a perfect, tiny life held in his hands.

Brandon shook his head, looking dismayed.

"He just won't settle. He's never like this normally. He tends to sleep pretty well at nighttime. But I'm trying to feed him from his bottle and he won't take it. He wants his mom…"

Olivia's stomach twisted. Her gut instinct was changing by the minute. Seeing Brandon now, oblivious to their suspicions, struggling to calm his child, it felt wrong to accuse him of anything. But it was their job to ask all the right questions, to expect the worst of people. He'd lied to them more than once. It was time to find out why.

"Brandon… we need to know why you lied to us," Olivia said, standing her ground. Brandon's head snapped up, and his forehead creased.

"Huh? What are you talking about?"

"You lied to us earlier. Twice. You weren't having lunch with your co-workers at all. You were seen with another woman at the restaurant, on a date. You were cheating on your wife, and you conveniently forgot to tell us about it. You have to understand this looks bad for you."

Brandon looked genuinely shocked that he'd been figured out. Olivia supposed that his exhaustion was catching up to him. Callum wailed even louder and Brandon shushed him, rubbing his back.

"I know, son. I know, Daddy has been a bad person. I know, you're disappointed in me," Brandon murmured with his eyes closed. Then he took a deep breath and looked up at Olivia and Brock.

"I'll come clean. But one thing I need you to know is… I never wanted to hurt Kristen. I would… I would *never* want that. I guess maybe this was my way of making sure that nothing else went wrong."

"Then why all of this, if you didn't want to hurt her?" Brock asked. "You already betrayed her."

THE **HOUSEWIFE**

"She betrayed me first," Brandon whispered. He sighed, rocking Callum back and forth to quiet him a little. "You've got to understand something... Kristen was perfect in so many ways. She was a perfect mother. She was generous, charitable... but that's easy to do when you're rich. She got used to throwing money at a problem. But one thing she wasn't so good at... was not getting exactly what she wanted, when she wanted it. And marriage was something she couldn't fix with money."

"What are you referring to?" Olivia asked. Brandon chewed his lip.

"She had this friend... Tom. A big burly guy, handsome, charming... They dated briefly in high school together, before I knew her. And he was always hanging around. I never liked him much... I guess he made me feel small. And I could never quite let go of the fact that once, she was his. He touched her the way I did, wanted all the things that me and Kristen now had together... and he was on her level, you know? He had money, status, looks. I could see something between them that was unspoken, but obvious. I knew that neither of them truly let go of the thing between them... and while I was jealous, I understood it. Because... well, I was in the same position."

Brock seemed like he wanted to say a thousand things, but all he said was, "And who was she?"

Brandon took a breath. "Marianne... the woman I was with at the restaurant... She was my first love. She moved to Australia for a year, and in that time, I met Kristen. And the thing is, I loved Marianne, but nothing had ever really happened between us. It was like a string of missed opportunities for our entire friendship. Something always stood in our way. And even when she came home, I buried my lingering feelings for her, because I loved Kristen too. Out of respect to her, I made my choice. Kristen was the one. I expected her to do the same with Tom, even if I never asked her out loud. For the sake of us, and our future. I thought that would be enough to make sure that we stayed solid."

"But she cheated on you first," Brock finished for Brandon. Pain crossed his face. He swallowed, bowing his head a little.

"It was just before we found out we were pregnant. She spent a drunken night with Tom that changed everything. I didn't want to let her go, but I was never that kind of man… the man who told her what to do all the time. I thought I could trust her, even if I couldn't trust him. The next day… she came home late. She was gone for hours and I couldn't get in contact with her. I was worried sick. But she showed up eventually, crying like she was the one about to get hurt. And then she admitted that she slept with him."

"And that made you furious," Olivia supplied.

"I had every right to be! She had betrayed my trust. I wanted nothing to do with her. And I guess my own walls caved in too… I let go of my morals in my anger. So I drove to stay with Marianne for a few days, to get my head together… but my bitterness changed things. I thought… If Kristen isn't holding back from Tom anymore, then why can't I have Marianne? Why can't I be with both? So one thing led to another. I'm not proud of it… but once I'd been with Marianne once, I couldn't… I just couldn't stop. Even after Kristen and I decided to work on our marriage, to choose one another for good… she said she'd stop seeing Tom, and I think that she did. But I didn't stop seeing Marianne. I felt… I felt more myself with her than I did with Kristen. It was so comfortable, so familiar… I didn't have to think about money all the time, didn't have Rebecca hanging over me, didn't have all this guilt of not being good enough… Marianne never made me feel less than I am. So I kept going back to her… like a moth to a flame."

Brandon took a deep breath, looking harrowed by his own tale. "There were so many complications in my marriage with Kristen. We even fought over whether Callum was mine or not. And I think she knew that I was lying to her for months…"

"You weren't at a conference yesterday, were you?" Brock asked. "I didn't find any information about it."

Brandon groaned. "That's just the place I used to park to go and see Marianne. I knew that Kristen would check on my location, that she'd do exactly what you did earlier today… so I'd park there and have Marianne pick me up for our dates together.

THE **HOUSEWIFE**

I… I wanted to spend Valentine's Day with her, even if only for a few hours. So we went for lunch, then back to her place to… well, you know. Then the rest is true. I went back to my car and drove home. I found Kristen there… and… oh, God…"

Callum continued to cry loudly and tears rolled down Brandon's cheeks too. He struggled for breath as he sobbed.

"We had a lot of issues, but I still loved her. I was just angry, and Marianne… Well, I love her too. It was messy and complicated, but I thought… I thought I had it figured out. But if I'd come home sooner… Maybe Kristen would still be alive. Maybe everything would be okay… "

Olivia didn't know how to comfort him. But she believed him. She understood how complicated marriages could be. She didn't think she could do what Brandon and Kristen had done to one another, but she also knew that boundaries could be stretched, bent, broken. And as she watched Brandon break down in front of her, she knew they'd been right about everything, but one small detail. Yes, he was a liar. Yes, he was a cheat and he'd done bad things.

But he wasn't a killer.

"I know things look bad for me," Brandon sniffed. "But I couldn't afford to tell you the truth. Not outright, not with everything going on. If Rebecca ever found out… she was already suspicious of me. She will do anything to take me down now, to make sure Callum and I are left out in the cold. Tom was the son-in-law she always wanted… I think she would've happily allowed me to leave Kristen for Marianne so that she could have the happy family she desired. I think she secretly hoped that Callum *was* Tom's. But I considered leaving Kristen… I never wanted to. She was my wife. And that meant something to me, even if I made a mess of it in the end." He paused, looking up at Olivia. "You can judge me. I understand. But I just need you to know… I wouldn't hurt her. I could never lay a hand on her. It's just not in my nature. And now… I just want to be here for my son. To start over."

Olivia nodded. There was nothing more for them there. Now that they had the complete picture of Brandon's life, it was an imperfect mess, but it had nothing to do with Kristen's death. In a strange way, she pitied the man. She didn't exactly feel sympathy for him, given that many of his problems were entirely of his own making, but that didn't mean that he deserved for his life to fall apart like this.

"Thank you for finally being honest with us," Brock said. "We'll find who did this. You take care of your son… take time to grieve… and if you think of anything, please call us."

Brandon was barely listening. He held his son close and wept as Olivia and Brock let themselves out of the hotel room. Olivia sighed.

"Well, that's one door closed."

Brock put his arm around her waist and guided her away. "Don't worry. Tomorrow we'll open another one."

CHAPTER NINE

Another door opened for Olivia and Brock after lunch the following day.

Olivia was preparing to continue their investigation into what might have happened to the security system in Kristen's home when Brock received a call from the local police. Olivia watched his face turn solemn as he listened to what the officer had to say. Olivia knew that it was often a bad sign when the police called them during an investigation. After all, they'd never once called to say they'd caught the culprit.

Brock nodded along to everything the officer was saying.

"Okay. Understood. Do you have the address? You'll text it? Okay, great. Thank you." Brock ended the call and turned to Olivia. "There's been another murder. Well, two, actually."

"*Two?*"

"In the same household. Karen Young and her wife, Nell Young. Thirty-four and twenty-nine years old. Both of them were repeatedly stabbed to death in their home, just like Kristen was. Their security systems were down and they also live in an expensive house. The police are yet to discover if anything has been stolen, but it seems likely that this is the same person we're dealing with."

"So much for Tom the scorned lover," she groaned. "Is this a serial killer now?"

"Seems so."

Olivia nodded, a little dazed by the revelation. Everything about it was too coincidental for it to be a different killer—same area, same class of people, all of them young, affluent women who might be vulnerable if home alone. If anything had been stolen, then it would solidify the case even further. But it also made things much more complicated. If there was more than one killing, then perhaps the crime wasn't as personal as Olivia had been led to believe. What was the connection between Karen and Nell Young with Kristen? Was it simply that they happened to be rich women? Was someone out to get what they had?

Or was there a deeper connection that they didn't know about yet?

One thing was for sure—their killer worked fast. They were only just starting to get started on Kristen's investigation, and now there were two more victims to consider. Olivia wasn't sure she had ever known a killer to work faster, and certainly not without assistance. Olivia began to wonder if there was any chance the killer had help of some sort—taking down two women at once was a feat in itself. But it wasn't impossible, and they already knew that their killer was smart, a boundary pusher, a quick hand. They couldn't dismiss this. They needed to get to the scene and learn more.

Olivia and Brock turned immediately from their route on the way to interview Tom and headed straight to the home of Karen and Nell Young, making it there within an hour of the phone call. The house was already cordoned off with police tape, and a

THE **HOUSEWIFE**

small crowd of neighbors had gathered around out of curiosity. Olivia knew that this kind of killing would cause unrest among the rich communities close by. They paid for their safety with high-tech alarm systems, bodyguards and big metal gates. When all that failed to keep them safe, how were they supposed to protect themselves? They were left vulnerable, just like any other person. Except that in an eat-the-rich society, they were more desirable targets.

Inside the house, Olivia was immediately met with a horrific scene. The two women lay face down in the front hallway, blood staining their pearly cream carpet red. Olivia took a step closer to see the damage. Once again, they'd been viciously stabbed. There were so many holes in their backs that it was like a disturbing dot-to-dot puzzle. The two women were lying close to one another like one had tried to save the other. It didn't look as though they'd tried to run, and if they had, they certainly hadn't made it very far. What had they done to deserve such a brutal death?

"Initial thoughts?" Brock asked. Olivia chewed her lip.

"Well... first off, I want to know... did they have any connection to Kristen? And secondly... did they use the same security company? Because if they did, then maybe we're looking for someone who works for the security companies. It's one thing that might connect them all."

"It's worth finding out. Something is not right with the security thing. These things are built to withstand anything. You can't just switch it off. And to commit two separate crimes pretty much back-to-back... they're not messing around. I wonder how long they've been building up to this."

Olivia shook her head, shocked at the brazen nature of it all. The killer had to be pretty bold—they were targeting high-profile people in high-security places. Their confidence in getting things done was almost bordering on cockiness. Perhaps that would trip them up eventually, but for now, they were killing at alarming speed.

Which meant that Olivia and Brock were against the clock.

"I'll bet these women were similar to Kristen. They could've had any number of staff traipsing through here. All with keys to the home, most likely. If the killer could handle that part, all they'd need to do would be to disable the security systems…"

"That's easier said than done. It's one thing to know the code for the front door alarm… but even that beeps when you enter the home, which would notify their presence. No… whoever did this switched off *everything,* and they did it in advance. The cameras being switched off is crucial to them getting away with this, and from what the police told me, the security system has been off for at least twelve hours. This likely happened last night. And it looks like they'd maybe just got home from somewhere, given that they're in the hallway. Which means the killer could have been waiting for them in the house."

"This killer doesn't waste even a second," Olivia murmured. Kristen was barely cold and now two more women had joined her. She straightened up. "We need to speak with the families of the victims."

"They're on their way. Apparently, Karen's parents died a few years back, but Nell's mother and father are coming over. Perhaps they'll have some insight as to who would want them dead and why."

∽

"I can't believe my baby Nellie is gone," Janice Young whispered, dabbing at her eyes. Her husband, Liam, put his arm around her, his face solemn. The couple sat in the sitting room of the police station, both of them looking completely worn out and defeated.

"I'm so sorry for your loss," Olivia said gently. "Were you close with your daughter?"

"Well… we had a somewhat difficult relationship these past few years, I'll admit," Janice said. "I hope you won't judge us… but it took us longer than it should for us to come to terms with our daughter's… choices."

THE **HOUSEWIFE**

"You mean in marriage?" Brock asked plainly. They didn't have time to beat around the bush, and whatever this family's issues were, they needed them aired, even if it put Janice and Liam in a poor light. Janice bowed her head a little.

"I know that it shouldn't matter, if she wanted to marry a woman. I suppose that's her choice."

"Not a choice. Being gay isn't a choice. She was born that way," Brock said firmly, his brow furrowed. Janice swallowed.

"Well… I know that now. I suppose love is love, isn't it? But it wasn't easy for us to understand, to try and see it from her perspective. Liam and I, we grew up in very traditional households…"

"We still loved her. She just didn't see it that way," Liam said, a tinge of bitterness in his tone. "I mean of course we loved her! We didn't always approve of her choices, but that's life. Anyway… since she and Karen married a few years back, we've not been in contact very much. Her choice, not ours. We tried to build bridges, but I think she'd decided to cut us out entirely. She wouldn't even let me walk her down the aisle on her wedding day."

"I think we were lucky to even be invited to the ceremony, honestly," Janice said with a pained smile. "Our daughter is very… headstrong. She gets that from me. She rarely goes back on her decisions. I imagine Karen didn't help our case. I'm convinced that she didn't like us from the very start."

"So I don't suppose you knew much about the life they led here? About who might've wanted to do this to them, or who might've had access to the house? That's what we're looking to find out," Olivia asked. Janice frowned.

"No, we didn't know what our daughter did every hour of every day. That's not unusual. And yes, maybe we had less access to her life than most parents… but you make it sound like we were bad parents… she pushed *us* away."

"My apologies, I wasn't trying to imply that," Olivia said, not wanting to get on the wrong side of Janice. "I just meant that the inner workings of their household might not be something you can enlighten us to. Is that correct?"

Janice shuffled uncomfortably. "Well... she didn't make it easy for us to keep connected with her life. We spoke on the phone once a month, but usually only for ten minutes or so. And in fact... we never visited her. She never gave her address to us. She said she might allow us to visit someday when trust was rebuilt... but we've... never even been inside our daughter's home." Janice's face crumpled. "I can't believe it. I can't believe it turned out this way."

Olivia handed Janice another tissue, which she took gratefully, but Olivia was already considering how they could leave as soon as possible. Olivia was fully aware that the parents were a dead end at this point. How would they be able to tell them anything about Nell when they'd been completely shut out of her life? It wasn't looking promising for leads, but Olivia knew there were other ways to figure out the story of the Young wives. It would simply take longer, and that worried Olivia. In the time it took for them to figure it out, another woman might be dead. They needed to figure out the pattern and get ahead of the killer's games before anyone else got hurt.

"We'll have to spend some time looking into your daughter's life at home before we can figure out who did this," Olivia told Janice and Liam. "In the meantime, if you can think of anything that might help, or anyone who might've wanted to hurt them..."

Janice sighed mournfully. "The world is out to get women like my daughter, Agent. It just isn't built for people like her."

"You might be right, in some ways. There's a lot of cruelty in the world. But I think Nell was accepted in her circles, at home, at work. Given the evidence, I don't think this was a hate crime," Olivia said. "I think whoever did this was a sick, twisted individual. I don't think they discriminate. I think they simply want to kill."

CHAPTER TEN

"**O**LIVIA... I THINK I MIGHT'VE FOUND SOMETHING of interest. Something the police haven't picked up on."

Olivia's ears pricked up. She and Brock were working from their hotel room, trying to rifle through the documents of Kristen and the Young family and find comparisons in their cases. So far, they'd been unsuccessful in finding a connection, though they were barely getting started. All the connections they'd tried so far—mistress Marianne, ex-boyfriend Tom, all the coworkers and close friends of all three victims—hadn't panned out. Still, it was music to Olivia's ears to hear that Brock might have found something so soon.

"What is it?"

"There was another case, about twenty miles from here… it took place three weeks ago. The victim was stabbed repeatedly, and their security system was disabled before it happened. So not only do we have a possible serial killer on the loose, but they've struck before. And not too long ago. I think they even did it a little further afield to stop the police from catching on to the connection right away."

Olivia shook her head. "This *has* to have some connection… It's too much of a coincidence. The whole business of the security going down is too similar. But how did the killer decide on the victim? Twenty miles is quite far away considering that the other two killings took place within two miles of one another. You're sure the victim had a security system?"

"Yes. There's an article about it in the local paper. It says that the victim, Kayla Mansfield, won the lottery last year and moved into a mansion with her boyfriend. She splashed out on a new car too, which was left in the driveway, but a bunch of other trinkets seemed to be missing. The boyfriend was the one who found her and reported it to the police. There was some speculation about whether her friend was involved, since she'd been at the house earlier in the day, but she had an alibi. Then there's the possibility of family involvement. At the same time of her lottery win, she cut ties with her family, presumably to avoid having to share her winnings."

"Cold, but interesting. That's the second victim that has cut ties with their family. Perhaps the killer is aware of this. Perhaps we shouldn't be looking at a family member, but someone who was aware of their situations. They might have figured out that they're isolated and vulnerable with less people checking up on them."

"It's a valid thought. No doubt the killer isn't fazed by a challenge, given that they're disabling entire security systems in order to get to their victims, but I suppose that's easier to do when the victims are likely to be alone in a big house with plenty of nooks and crannies. It also says here in the article that their security company made a statement, denying accountability for what had happened. I imagine that didn't go over well for them."

THE **HOUSEWIFE**

"It's certainly not good for business. Does it say which company was used? Maybe it matches up to the ones that our other victims used?" Olivia asked.

"It's called Techtite Locks. I don't think either of the other victims used it."

"No, they've all used different companies so far. So whoever the killer is must be really good at wiping out security. They've managed to take on three different ones in the space of a month and get away with it."

Brock huffed. "You'd think they'd aim a little bigger with this kind of prowess… they could be robbing banks with this level of skill. Why stop at stealing designer handbags and killing unassuming rich women?"

"I don't think it's about the monetary value of what they steal… I guess it must just be the thrill of it. But it got me thinking… this whole thing feels like it's performed with a practiced hand. Three successful murders, pretty much back-to-back… and a flawless execution, pardon the pun. So where has this killer suddenly popped up from? Did they have previous experience of killing, or are they just *that* good?"

"No one is just good at it," Brock countered. "It must take practice, nerve, planning. Maybe even a few messy first tries, which could be why their other killings don't match up to exactly what we're looking for."

"You think the killer had a few trial runs?"

"Quite possibly. I mean, stabbings don't take much skill, anyone with a big knife could get away with that… but it's the rest of it that interests me. The art of not being caught. I think we should take the search a little wider and see if there are any similar cases in a wider radius. Maybe the killer has to keep on the run, moving around and changing methods to avoid being detected."

Olivia nodded. "Good idea. Let's dig around, see what else we can find. Who knows… if the killer was a little clumsier earlier in their career, then maybe we can find out more about who we are dealing with. There might be some evidence to pick up on, or a flaw in their handiwork."

The search was on. Olivia and Brock sat down together to take a wider look at the surrounding states. They expanded the search throughout the DMV area, but found nothing of a similar MO. They took their time, looking for cases that involved stabbings or disabled security, but there wasn't anything that felt relevant. They moved on to the Carolinas and West Virginia, but again, they came up blank.

"Do you think maybe our search is too general? Should we just be looking for killings with the exact same MO?" Olivia said. "The style is pretty distinctive, considering that the killing itself isn't skilled in any form. I feel like without the security hack and the robberies, this could be performed by anyone."

"That's exactly why we should be looking at *all* cases."

Olivia groaned. "We'll be here forever. That can't be it."

"But we have to broaden the search. Maybe the killer likes to change things up every now and then. If they really are as smart as we believe they are, it could be deliberate to throw the police off the scent," Brock pointed out. "And besides, killers take time to hone their craft. Maybe they were just finding their feet before, trying to find their style. If they take pride in their work, then it's unlikely they'll change it up when they're finally coming into the spotlight."

"This thing with the security, though… it's not something that just *anyone* can jump on board with, right? It's no simple task to break into a house without triggering a complex alarm system, but to disable it too? They know exactly where their strengths lie. If they really are a serial killer and it went beyond what we've seen here, then I feel like they will be using this to their advantage wherever they go. And we have to look again at our victims… there is one thing that connects all of them. They are all privileged white women with lots of money. One of them was a mother, but it feels like the focus is more on their status. It could be jealousy driving the killer, but it could also be a power play. So many male killers like to humiliate women, to show that they have something over them… and in this case, I think we're looking for someone who wants to prove that, despite their humble background, they can still take down the rich. They can still prove that they can take down any woman they want to, rich or not."

THE **HOUSEWIFE**

"I hear you, and I think you're probably right. But if we don't widen the search, we might miss something, and I don't want to risk that. Let's keep looking for a little longer with a wider scope. It'll help us think outside of the box."

They continued to search through the nearby states. Olivia felt a little overwhelmed by the amount of cases that were coming up on the search. Their killer was quick and efficient, for sure, but how many people had they killed before? With so many violent stabbings taking place across the country, the number could be in the dozens. Or it could be only a handful. Who knew what their killer was capable of, after all they'd pulled off so far?

And then there was something that worried her even more—they had only just begun to consider nearby states. What if the killer had taken their work further afield, far from the confines of the East Coast? They might even try further afield if they could. At the rate of their killings so far, it felt like anything was possible. Who would be next, and where would the killer strike? Time was a weight on Olivia's shoulders, and she could feel it slipping away from her far too quickly.

"Hey, what about this? I think this could be significant… "

Olivia checked out what Brock was looking at. Atlantic City, New Jersey, only a few hours north of Melrose. An aspiring starlet had been killed in her hotel room at the Palazzo during a power outage. She had been stabbed multiple times after the power cut caused the key card mechanism on her door to fail and the killer walked straight in, unseen by the cameras because of the power cut. Olivia nodded slowly as she read the story.

"Yes… this feels relevant. Another well-off white woman, staying in a fancy hotel. Another woman staying on her own, making her a vulnerable target. The killer used a power cut to their advantage, knowing the cameras would be off, knowing what they'd get away with… it's riskier, given that anyone in a nearby room could've heard the commotion… but the killer clearly knew what they were doing, because it looks like they got away without anyone even knowing they were there…"

"Until the cleaning crew found the woman dead in her room," Brock finished up. "It all seems to line up. This might be our killer.

And they're not afraid of the scale of their kills… they're good at it. And they're smart… never staying in one place too long. I bet we don't have long now until they move on again. Either to another kill in town or to a new location."

"At least that tells us a little about the killer… someone who has experience in security or hacking, someone with a high IQ, someone who bounces around and perhaps can't hold a job down for very long… it's not much, but if we can build on what we know, the picture of our killer is going to start looking a lot more clear."

"Then we know what we need to do. Let's dig around a little more. We need to find more cases, more correlations. Something to create a pattern."

"Rich white women," Olivia said glumly. "Not exactly the most specific place to look."

"But it is a place to look," Brock offered.

"Why don't you keep on that, then. I'll start digging into the security companies the victims used and try to find if any person can be linked to all three. Maybe an ex-employee, someone who knew how to disable the system. And then I want to look more specifically at who exactly had access to each of the houses of our main victims. If we can find the link, we can find the killer."

CHAPTER ELEVEN

"THESE WOMEN REALLY HAD PEOPLE MOVING THROUGH their houses like it was a train station," Brock commented as he wrote down another name from the Young family's hire list. So far, they hadn't come up with any matches in correlation to Kristen's trusted contacts, but Olivia and Brock had been working on the list for several hours, and the list just kept growing. "The Young family had a masseuse coming to their home three times a week, plus a physical therapist several times a week for Nell. Every Saturday, they booked a hair stylist and makeup artist to come over and get them ready for their evening… but they didn't go out. Oh, no. They had a private chef come to their house and cook for them."

Olivia whistled. "I guess I'd be a homebody too if I had a house as stunning as theirs," she said. "And I guess they felt safe in their home. They trusted the people they were letting into their home… but it was likely one of them that let them down in the end."

"We're saying that, but there's not a single person on Nell and Karen's list that matches with Kristen's, so I don't know whether we're going to find a correlation there. She had a lot fewer people coming in, actually. There were all of the nannies that she ended up sending away… but Brandon told us that she gave them big payouts and glowing references when they left her service, so I can't see there being any bad blood there. It doesn't exactly seem like the kind of thing that would inspire murder, anyway. But other than that, it was mostly people who were helping around the house… the maid, the gardener…"

"Brandon did say that the gardener had a thing for Kristen…"

"Okay, sure, that could be of interest, except that we can't connect him to the Young family. I mean, we haven't even started looking at Kayla Mansfield's list yet, but even if there is one match there, how do we then connect it back to Nell and Karen?"

"We'll cross that bridge when we get to it. We'll just have to keep hoping that we make some kind of match along the way."

But another hour later, there was still no visible connection between the four victims. They didn't share any of the same staff, and any one-time hires they'd made were also unrelated to the three households as a whole. It was frustrating, but unsurprising to Olivia. She felt like whoever they were dealing with was a little too clever to be caught on the payroll of all of their victims. Whoever it was, she felt that there was something more clever to them. Planning a murder was one thing, but planning to tear down walls of security first to get to them? That was another level. That was calculation.

"I just keep coming back to the security systems," Olivia said as she swirled cream into her coffee, desperate for a caffeine boost. "It's got to be relevant."

"None of the victims used the same security company, though. We already checked that."

THE **HOUSEWIFE**

"Sure, but whoever we're looking for seems pretty adaptable, so long as they have something to work with. I can't say I know much about that kind of thing, but there's got to be a core to all of these security systems that's similar, right? The killer clearly knew how to deal with all of them, so either they had prior knowledge of each system, or they just knew how to deal with this kind of thing in general. And if they really know what they're doing, perhaps they can take the systems down remotely, so they could take it down before they even entered the property. Hence why Kristen's systems went down after Brandon left the house, but we didn't see anyone nearby on the footage we have before the blackout. The killer clearly planned this out meticulously. They switched the systems off in Kristen's home the moment that Brandon left the house, pretty much. The killer was watching, learning over a period of time. They likely knew everything about the family before they went in for the kill."

"You think the women were stalked beforehand?"

"Oh, absolutely. It's all a part of the thrill, right? And to pull this off, the killer must've been aware of the routines of the victims. I mean, Kristen's schedule was pretty consistent, from what Brandon told us. She went to the same classes every week, took Callum to the same park every day, and stopped for breakfast in the same patisserie each morning... She was a creature of habit, which was likely what made her the perfect target for the killer. She was announcing exactly where she'd be and when through her routines. So picture it—she leaves the house to take Callum to the park, like Brandon said she would have done that day. The killer takes down the security and makes it inside the house while she's gone, so nobody notices what's happened. Then all they have to do is wait for an opportune moment. Kristen returns home. She thinks it's a little strange that the house alarm didn't trigger, perhaps, but she's preoccupied with her kid so she forgets, or plans to go back to it later. The killer waits for her to put Callum down for a nap, and then bingo... She heads into the kitchen, headphones in, paying no mind to her surroundings. She's relaxed, as she should be. She believes she's safe inside her home. She's then easy to sneak up on..."

"Before she knows what's happening, before she's even noticed the security is down, she's dead," Brock finished. "All because the killer knew exactly how she'd act on the day."

Olivia nodded. "And then take Nell and Karen… a little more difficult. I mean, there were two of them to take down, and they had a constant rotating door of guests and staff. But the killer knew that. They knew the gaps in the schedule. And that's when they chose to strike. The killer had already been watching them, had already been monitoring their schedule, before they even killed Kristen. They struck while the police were distracted. Which means they probably have a list of victims they're checking off."

Olivia finished up, feeling a little breathless after weaving her version of events. Brock blinked at her several times.

"That's a lot of information to take in at once, Olivia."

"Exactly. It's a lot for *us*… we're still playing catch up to the killer. This is our job and it's still a lot to handle in one day. But their pre-planning prepared the killer for the chaos of the last few days. I think they knew exactly how much this would throw us off. And who knows. If the pattern continues, they have another house on their hit list right now. If they have any sense, they'll lay low for a little while, but who knows. They've killed four people in a short space of time. Another kill isn't so much of a stretch."

Brock sighed. "Based on our theories, they could be halfway to another state by now. That is, if they're hopping around the country."

"Possibly. But they must've been in town for a little while. The killing in Atlantic City was six months ago. We didn't see any others taking place in that time, though admittedly we still have a lot of searching to do… but maybe we're looking at it wrong. Maybe the killer lives around here, but it's their first time killing on home turf. We've been assuming that they move around a lot, but what if their usual MO is that they leave town to make a kill somewhere anonymous, somewhere they have no connections? This town couldn't be more different from Atlantic City. We only looked further afield because it's our job to think outside of the box. This killer seems to be calculated, but driven by a thrill. And what's more thrilling for a killer than stalking and killing someone

THE **HOUSEWIFE**

that you pass on the street every day? It must make the killer feel powerful..."

"I guess... but isn't working close to home a little dangerous? Even for someone who has their head screwed on like our killer?"

"But think about it... you're the killer. It's the only thing that gets you out of bed in the morning. You love it. You love the preparation, you love knowing you'll have blood on your hands by the end of it. But it's not enough anymore. Taking trips out of town every now and then to make a kill just doesn't do it for you anymore. And then you're out one morning, going about your day, and you see this woman. She's beautiful and at ease, in a way only rich women can be. You can sense it on her, and she's exactly your type. Killing wise, of course. And it gets you thinking... you live surrounded by women like her. You could pass her every day on the street and it wouldn't be suspicious... you live in the same town, after all. She's oblivious to your intentions, because why would she suspect anything of you? She doesn't even notice you, you're invisible to her. She lives in a world of her own where you just don't make the cut. Maybe that angers you a little and you want to make yourself known to her in some way. And you realize that you're smart enough to get away with more... to take things to the next level. You can become a part of her life without her even noticing, and then take her down when she's least expecting it. If I was the killer, I don't think there would be anything more thrilling. Reading in the local newspaper about how women are dropping like flies, and it's all because of you. Blending into the background because on the surface you're charming, a good neighbor, you pay your taxes and you keep to yourself. No one knows this other side to you... and you're perfectly capable of pulling it off. And so ambition finally takes over. This is what you've been waiting for all along."

Brock let out a long breath. "Wow. When you put it like that... I guess that makes a lot of sense. Kind of creepy how much you got into that, though."

Olivia grinned and took a bow. "The performance of a lifetime, right? So, what do you think? Could I be right?"

"I mean, there's no harm in checking it out. What about the security companies?"

"Well, I thought about that too. This killer clearly knows their stuff, so let's assume they work for a security company, or at least did at some point, to gain that technical knowledge needed to pull this off. We have at least three companies that are local, each of them representing a different victim. If we do a deep dive, there might actually be more correlation between the three of them than we originally thought. Like, maybe the killer hired all three at some point and got to know their products well enough to be able to disable them… or better yet, the killer could've worked for them all, hopping between them. It might be a stretch… it could easily be any of the employees at any of the three. But if we start to dig, we can look for motive and means."

"Alright, boss. Since you're on a roll, I'll let you take the lead on this one," Brock said with a smile. "You know, you should do big speeches like that more often. It's kind of hot how much you got into it. I love the passion."

"Now you've got me blushing, Brock. If you get a list of Kayla's connections, that would be good. We might still have something left there."

The pair of them set to work. Olivia decided to call Kristen's security company first, considering that they knew the most about her case. She dialed the company number for StrongHold, waiting patiently for them to pick up.

"Hello, this is Cara from StrongHold Security. How may I help you today?"

"Hi, Cara. My name is Olivia Knight. I'm with the FBI and I'm calling about an investigation that I'm running into a series of murders. Could I speak to you for a moment about your employees?"

There was a short silence on the other end of the line. "I've been told not to speak with anyone about the ongoing case…"

"And why is that?"

"The Grace family… their daughter was one of the victims… they are currently attempting to sue, and anything we say could be used against us. I really shouldn't have said that, but I thought you should know why… but we will have to decline. I'm sorry."

Olivia sighed. She should have expected that Rebecca Grace would already be digging her claws in and causing trouble. She rubbed at her temple.

"Look, I'm not trying to put you in a bind or anything. I'm not just calling this company, I'm looking at two other security companies too. This isn't just about Kristen's case anymore, there are at least two other connected murders. We are hoping that we can find someone within the companies that connects them, to see if there's an employee behind all of this. It won't reflect on the company itself, I assure you."

Cara sighed, stress radiating from her tone. "I don't know… I'm just an assistant… I don't want to get anyone in trouble. Including myself."

"With all due respect, someone needs to be in trouble for what has happened. Someone is killing women, women in *your* town. Someone is actively disabling the security systems in all of these houses. It'll happen again if the killer isn't caught. We're looking at a possible former employee at your company. If StrongHold isn't seen to be cooperative, you'll all be in a lot more trouble, don't you think?"

Olivia felt guilty even as she said it out loud. She hated putting pressure on someone she didn't know, an assistant just trying to do as she was told. She certainly wasn't being paid enough to put her job on the line on Olivia's behalf. But they needed names, and the quicker StrongHold handed them over, the better it would be for everyone. Cara took a shaky breath on the other end of the line.

"What was it you wanted from us again?"

Olivia let out a quiet sigh of relief. She didn't want to walk away empty-handed from the call. Cara was her lifeline.

"I'm going to need a list of employees, past and present. In any department you might have, but definitely in the specialists who install the security systems. The people who would be going in and out of houses each day and having access to various properties."

"How far are you looking for us to date back?"

"I guess any time within the last ten years. I don't imagine we need to go so far back, but it's better to be safe than sorry."

"I'm not sure if we keep records from that far back… but I can check for you. Is that all you need from us?"

"Yes, that will do."

"And… I'm not going to get into trouble, am I? I really don't feel comfortable with this…"

"Cara, you've done nothing wrong. If there's any foul play involved, it will be the individual responsible that pays for it, not the company. If you get any flack from your bosses, direct them to me. And I assure you, Rebecca Grace won't hear a word about this conversation. I don't want her hearing about this any more than you do."

The woman sighed. "Alright… I guess that makes me feel a little better. Do you have an email I can forward the documents to? And some way to check the credibility of this call and the forwarding address?"

"No problem. And yes, this call is coming from my work phone. You can check it with the local FBI field office for legitimacy, as with my email address. I'm happy to wait while you do your checks."

"That's alright… I'll get back to you when I'm satisfied. Thank you for your call. StrongHold wishes you a pleasant day."

Olivia rattled off her details to Cara and then the pair of them ended the call. Olivia had to hope that Cara would go through with her promise. If she didn't, their job was about to get a lot more difficult.

"One down, two to go," she murmured to herself.

"Olivia… you'll have to go back to that later. I think I've got something. Something we almost missed," Brock said from across the room.

"Really?" Olivia said, turning around in her seat to face him. "What is it?"

"Brandon told us that there were a number of nannies that Kristen got through, right? He said that she dismissed all of them."

"Yeah, but I thought it was all amicable?"

"Supposedly it was. But I'm looking at Kayla's list, and they hired the same nanny at a point in time. Her name was Pixie Prentiss."

"Wow, really?"

"Yep. Quite a name, right? But that's not the most interesting thing about her."

"Do tell."

"Not only did both Kristen and Kayla hire her… they also both fired her."

CHAPTER TWELVE

AFTER THE DISCOVERY THAT BOTH KAYLA AND KRISTEN had hired Pixie as a babysitter, there was only one person they could speak to aside from the woman herself. In the interest of learning more first, they had to call on the one person who might be able to give them the full story.

"Am I in trouble?" Brandon asked as he picked up the phone. "I swear, I've been honest about everything else…"

"You're not in trouble, Brandon. We just have some questions about the people who came into your employment while your wife was alive."

"Oh," Brandon said with a tired sigh of relief. Olivia could hear Callum fussing in the background. No doubt Brandon was

THE **HOUSEWIFE**

still suffering from exhaustion. "Are you able to come to me? I don't think I'm in a state to drive."

Olivia agreed that they would meet him at the hotel again. When they arrived, he was still looking a little worse for wear, unshowered and still in his pajamas, but considering his circumstances, Olivia thought he was doing well. He was clutching a baby monitor in his hand as he led them to the elevator.

"I'm happy to talk to you considering that it must be important, but you're going to have to keep the noise down, if that's okay? I finally got Callum to settle down. It's been a nightmare. I've barely slept."

"Don't worry, we won't keep you long," Brock assured him. "But this *is* important."

"What is this about, then? The gardener? Because I know I gave him a bit of stick before, but I really don't think he would hurt Kristen…"

"No, not him. This is about Pixie Prentiss."

Brandon's eyes widened a little. "Oh. I see…"

"I know you probably don't want us digging up the past, considering that you and Kristen fired her… but this could be important. Pixie Prentiss is the only person we have that connects your wife to the other recent victims in the area. It could be our first real lead."

"Well… if I'm going to have to talk about Pixie, then I hope it helps your investigation. I've been hoping to forget about her, to be honest. I'm sure you'll understand why soon enough."

They entered the hotel room as quietly as they could. Brandon sat down on the bed, his shoulders slumped forward.

"Okay. What do you want to know?"

"Well, anything you can tell us about why you let her go," Olivia said. "I know that your wife dismissed all of her nannies eventually, but it seems this one was for a reason."

Brandon sighed. "Well, it wasn't my wife that dismissed Pixie at all. It was me."

Olivia raised an eyebrow. "Oh? And did you have a reason for letting her go?"

Brandon scoffed. "You could say that. I didn't trust Pixie from the moment I met her. She was the fourth sitter we hired from the agency that Kristen used. There was nothing wrong with the agency, but as I told you, Kristen was fussy about who she would trust around Callum, and with good reason. Before Pixie, Kristen had picked older women to help out, more matronly types, but something wasn't working for her, so she decided to try something different. She hoped that someone young and fun might help. With everything going on around us, Kristen had a lot of dips in her mood and she got depressed. You know, the way women often do after pregnancy… I forget what the doctors called it now."

"Postpartum depression," Olivia supplied.

"Yeah, that. Anyway, I think she hoped that having a girl like Pixie around would be good for her as well, especially while I was working and she was on her own all day. She would sometimes hire the sitters just to have somebody else in the house with her."

"So what was the issue? Did Kristen like her and you didn't?" Brock asked. Brandon wavered, shifting his eyes away from Brock.

"Sort of. Kristen was right in some ways… Pixie was different. She was pretty good with Callum, but there was something off about her. Something a little… manic. She wore wacky clothes and a lot of cheap perfume. She'd always be vaping in the backyard, even though I asked her not to bring that stuff to the house. And I doubt it was just nicotine if you get my drift. And she could be… inappropriate."

"Flirtatious?"

"You could definitely say that. Kristen always seemed to think I was overreacting if I commented on it, but she'd find excuses to touch me, saying suggestive things… I think she was teasing me to get a reaction out of me. Not the kind of behavior I wanted to see in someone taking care of my boy. I didn't understand the appeal, even though Kristen seemed taken by her. She didn't seem like the kind of girl you'd choose to look after your kid… but Kristen didn't mind, so I let it slide for a while. But then there was an… incident."

"Incident?"

THE **HOUSEWIFE**

Brandon shifted again, threading his fingers together. He couldn't look either of them in the eye. "How much detail do you want?"

"All of it, Brandon. No holding back this time, okay?"

Brandon puffed his cheeks out as he took in an unsteady breath. "Okay, okay, I can do this… well, Kristen had plans with an old girlfriend one day and decided that she was comfortable leaving Callum with Pixie, so she went on her way. She didn't often leave them on their own, she preferred to be hands-on with our son, but we both decided that it was good for her mental health to get out now and again. I tried to get Rebecca to take care of him for the day, but you can imagine how she spun that one… so in the end, I agreed that Pixie would have to do it. I couldn't take the time out of work and Kristen needed a break. So Pixie had Callum from ten in the morning, and I planned to cut out early to relieve her at four-thirty. But there was a power outage at the bank and we all got sent home early, which was great for me. I had plans to cook dinner for Kristen, to try and mend things between us a little. I was grateful for the extra time. But when I got home I heard… noises."

Olivia raised an eyebrow, but didn't say anything, encouraging Brandon to continue. She had to admit, she was interested to see how the story would play out. He looked uncomfortable as he took a deep breath.

"Pixie had expected us both to be out for longer, knowing I wasn't due back for another hour… and she'd invited company over. I walked through the kitchen and the fridge had been raided… all our food, they'd dug into it. And there was one of our bottles of wine we'd been saving on the counter, fully empty. I was mortified. I mean, I don't care about the price of things, but it's the principle of it! I knew she was willing to take liberties, but this was another level. I knew then that Pixie was even more trouble than I expected. And then I went upstairs and found her in my bed with her lover… wearing my wife's clothes… and when she spotted me, she just laughed and… and…"

"And?" Olivia prompted. Brandon swallowed.

"And asked if I'd like to join them. She was drunk. I don't know how she thought she was going to hide what she'd done before we got home… maybe she wasn't going to. Maybe she wanted to get caught. I don't know…"

"Wow," Brock said, blinking in surprise. "I wasn't expecting that. You fired her on the spot, I expect?"

Brandon nodded, his eyes on the floor. "I had to. I mean… young people make mistakes. I could've almost forgiven her if she wasn't supposed to be in charge of taking care of my son. He was fine… she had the baby monitor with her and he was sound asleep… but it was just disgusting behavior. I told her to leave and never come back, or I'd report her. I called the agency to tell them that the arrangement wouldn't work out and that I wouldn't give her a reference. For her own sake, I didn't say what had happened, hoping she would get her act together. Looking back, I wish that I had been honest."

"You tried to do a good thing, giving her a second chance," Olivia said. "What did Kristen think?"

Brandon shook his head. "I never told her what happened… I just let her believe that Pixie had left of her own accord. I wasn't going to let her anywhere near my son again… or my wife, even. Hell, I didn't want her anywhere near me either. I was glad to see the back of her. That was so completely unacceptable. I feel angry just talking about it, and it was months ago. But now I know I should have reported her anyway… to think she went on to do the same kinds of things in other people's houses… and now you think she's connected to the murder?"

"Well, we don't know that yet. It might be a stretch, we don't know much yet. But one of the other victims did hire her to look after her child, a couple of months after you let her go. And given her erratic behavior, it sounds like she's a troublemaker. We're going to have to speak to the agency that hired her and see if we can track her down. If she's been fired numerous times by different clients, I doubt she still works there, but we might be able to get an address for her," Olivia said.

She had considered trying to contact Kayla's family to ask if they knew anything about Pixie, but knowing that Kayla had cut off her parents following her lottery win, she didn't see much point. Now that they'd heard about Pixie's odd behavior from Brandon, they didn't need much more reason to track her down and speak to her. It was suspicious enough that she had done so many odd things and that she'd been fired. It gave her a motive, and if she'd been in the house before, perhaps she knew how to get in undetected.

"Well, I wish you luck. If she's as crazy as she was the last time I saw her, then I wouldn't put it past her to do something horrific. She was very strange. It was like she had no sense of right and wrong... she just followed her impulses, taking what she wanted, when she wanted it," Brandon said with a shudder. "I don't usually like to point fingers... but I'm glad you came to speak to me. I hadn't even considered her, given how long ago it was. But the more I think about it, the more of a bad feeling I've got about it."

Olivia nodded in understanding. A lack of empathy was common in psychopaths, and psychopaths were capable of terrible things as a result. It sounded like they were dealing with one in Pixie. Olivia supposed that it would've been possible for someone like her to have meddled with the security, maybe even kept a cut key from the houses she wanted to strike. By the sounds of it, she didn't have an issue with doing things that broke the mold or pushed boundaries. Was murder on her roster? Olivia didn't feel overly sure of the woman's capabilities, but she knew it was worth checking out.

"Thanks again for your help. We'll be in touch," Brock told Brandon. He raised an eyebrow.

"Again?"

"If necessary. You're our best source right now. But we'll try and give you some space. Try and get some sleep. I hear you're supposed to sleep while the baby sleeps."

Brandon offered a tired smile. "Thanks. I'll try."

Olivia and Brock left the room, shutting the door gently behind them. Olivia raised her eyebrow to Brock.

"Well, looks like we have a potential suspect. I'll call the agency."

"Perfect."

As they headed back to the car, Olivia dialed the number and put the phone to her ear. It took about twenty minutes fiddling with the number prompts and repetitive menu options to get to an actual human being.

"Tiny Tots, where care is our business! How might I help you today?"

"This is Agent Olivia Knight of the FBI. I'm calling to discuss one of your employees. Is there a manager available?" she asked curtly, irritated that she'd been run around for so long.

"Ma'am, I assure you all of our employees are of the highest quality, and they receive a thorough background check before they're hired …"

Olivia let out a breath. "Look, I'm sorry, I really do not want to blow up at you. Can you just put on a manager for me? It's a federal matter."

"Right. Um. I'll put you on a brief hold."

Some jaunty, upbeat music came over the line, which only irritated Olivia further. She gripped her phone tightly and stared straight ahead.

Brock looked over with a teasing smirk. "A federal matter?"

She made a face at him but couldn't come up with a comeback before the manager came to the line.

"Ma'am, this is the manager speaking. I assure you, if you've had an issue with one of our employees—"

"I appreciate the concern, but I'm not calling as a customer. I'm with the FBI. I'm calling to follow up with one of your employees by the name of Pixie Prentiss."

The woman on the other end sighed in recognition. Olivia noted that it might not have been the first time there had been a complaint lodged against her. "Oh, Pixie… yes, I know of her. She is no longer in our employment. Was let go some time ago, actually."

"Do you have any forwarding information regarding her? It's urgent to track her down as quickly as we can," Olivia said.

The manager balked at this. "I don't think I can provide that information."

THE **HOUSEWIFE**

"Look, I'm kind of in a bind here," Olivia pressed. "It's vital we track down Pixie. We're investigating a series of murders and she babysat for two of the victims."

The woman gasped. "Oh, my god! You don't think she—"

"I'm not saying she's definitely involved, but she's absolutely a person of interest in our case. If there's any information you can provide me at all, anything that might help, please. We need to know it."

"She, um… she seemed like a sweet girl when we took her on, no previous issues with the law, well qualified. Like all our employees, she passed her background check with flying colors. But I think one day, something snapped in her. It changed everything."

"What do you mean?"

"She got a new boyfriend… I don't remember his name, but he was a weirdo. He made me uncomfortable from the start. He dropped her off at the office a few times and I just really didn't like the sight of him. But she was so into him. She cut all of her hair off, got a bunch of tattoos and piercings… which wasn't an issue in itself, it was just a full one-eighty on how she was before. I don't like to judge… but honestly, some of our clients did. She lost some of her regulars, but she didn't seem to care. And then her behavior became… erratic. When we started having complaints about her we had to let her go. You can't have someone unstable around a child… I was never going to put anyone in danger for the sake of a young girl's first job. But I did worry about her. I suspect she was on drugs or something. People don't just change like that so suddenly… there was certainly more going on."

"I see. Well, do you have any information on how we can find her? Where was she living when she was in your employment? We really need to speak to her and see what went on."

"I'm not sure I should be giving you that information…"

"Ma'am, this is a murder investigation. We're not interested in anything, but finding out whether she killed the women in question. She had the motive and the means to hurt women, and there may be others on her list. We need to stop this before anyone else gets hurt. Please don't make me get a warrant."

"...very well. Let me find her address. It should still be on the database. I'll put you on a brief—"

"Please don't," Olivia said. "I can't stand that music. I'll just wait."

"Alright." Thankfully, the silence was brief as the manager called up the information.

"I don't know if she'll still be there... but I recall she changed her residence to her boyfriend's apartment, shortly before she was dismissed. You can find them in Point Plaza Apartments, unit 8. It's on Ashdale Road."

"Thank you. You've been a big help. I may need to follow up on this, but this is all for now. I appreciate your time."

"I hope you won't need to call again," the manager said stiffly.

Olivia ended the call with a sigh and turned to Brock.

"It's possible that she's still living in her boyfriend's apartment. But it sounds like both Pixie and her partner may be a little... unhinged. I think we need to be cautious about how we approach this. If we can get Pixie on her own, outside of the apartment, that might be the best option."

"I guess we'll just have to see when we get there. If she's on edge already, we might not have the luxury of choice," Brock said as he turned toward the apartment complex. "But we can cross that bridge when we get to it. Let's head there now and hope for the best."

CHAPTER THIRTEEN

ASHDALE ROAD WAS A FAR CRY FROM THE BEAUTY OF THE rest of the town, which was complete with its expensive housing and immaculate parks. Olivia felt safe on the whole, despite the string of murders that had taken place, and she knew that was something to do with the wealth of the area, almost paying off trouble.

This side of town, on the other hand, looked to be derelict and falling apart. There were some unfinished blocks of apartments that quickly descended into building sites that had never been returned to. It was clear that the area had been left alone and had invited trouble. Now, the debris was scattered with needles and abandoned beer cans that rattled in the wind. Olivia wondered what had happened there—most likely a fancy development project gone wrong. Perhaps they'd run out of funding and discarded the project like an unwanted toy. But she could now understand how Pixie might've ended up in such a place. Unable to work after being fired, living in her boyfriend's sketchy apartment, taking what she could get. It wasn't uncommon for women like her to end up on the wrong side of town.

Olivia had a bad feeling in the pit of her stomach—the entire place seemed shady and dangerous—but they couldn't turn back. They needed to find Pixie and figure out what her deal was. For now, she was the one string keeping all of their victims attached to one another.

"Are these even real apartments? They don't look like they're fit to live in," Brock asked as they pulled into the otherwise empty parking lot of Point Plaza. "Some of them look like they don't have any windows…"

"I guess this place has gone to ruin…" Olivia mused. "But that might be exactly why Pixie is staying here. It's a good place to stay off the radar."

"I guess the rent is cheap too. As in non-existent," Brock murmured. "I don't imagine anyone chooses to come to a place like this… but it doesn't mean that people don't."

They got out of the car and stared up at the building. It certainly wasn't fit for anyone to be living in, but she could hear music thumping from somewhere within the skeleton of a building, like the beating heart of the place. Olivia made sure her gun was securely holstered. The place was creepy, and she certainly wasn't going in there unarmed.

"Ready?" she asked Brock. He nodded solemnly and they headed for the staircase. There was a door frame without a door which they passed through, their footsteps echoing on the stone steps as they went up.

Olivia caught sight of Apartment 6, the number simply drawn next to the door on the concrete walls. The music they'd heard from the parking lot was coming from further down the hall. Olivia nodded for Brock to follow her and they crept closer to the sound.

THE **HOUSEWIFE**

There was a party going on, despite the fact they were in the middle of the day, the sun high in the sky. Two people stood outside the door, smoking cigarettes over the balcony that smelled like marijuana. Olivia wasn't concerned with the drugs on the premises though—they had more important things to investigate. Knowing she looked out of place, she lifted her chin and approached the smokers.

"I'm looking for Pixie. Pixie Prentiss. Is she around?" Olivia asked. A girl with a mohawk and a pierced brow smirked back at her. She was chewing a wad of pink gum that she swished around her mouth wetly, and all Olivia could think about was how bad it must taste if she was smoking at the same time.

"Pixie's always here. You can find her in the bathroom more often than not."

"Gross," Brock murmured. The girl rolled her eyes.

"She's not sitting on the can, dummy. It's just where she likes to hang out when she's off her face. You can see for yourself. Unless you're cops… you're not cops, are you?"

"Nah, we're here for the party," Brock said, straight-faced.

Olivia was fully aware that she didn't look like a party girl, and she never once had. That much had been proven at her school reunion. Still, the smokers seemed to take her word for it. They nodded absent-mindedly and then carried on their conversation, their voices drawling out like someone had put them on half speed. Olivia and Brock slipped into the apartment, heads high as though they belonged there.

No one paid them much mind, though it was clear they stuck out like sore thumbs. They were far too strait-laced to ever fit in, but it didn't matter. Everyone around them was too far gone to notice. Olivia moved slowly through the place, unsure who she was looking for. The one thing they didn't have was a picture of Pixie to identify her. But when she heard laughter echoing in a room to her left, she figured she must have found the bathroom. The door was ajar, so she pushed it gently to open it.

The girl sitting in the bath was alone. There was no water in the tub—Olivia doubted running water was available in the squat—but there was a pool of acidic-smelling beer at the girl's bare feet. Her toes were painted a deep purple and she swirled her big toe in the pool of beer. The rim of the tub was lined with stubbed-out cigarettes arranged neatly like dominos, and the smell of them clung to the walls.

The girl herself looked a mess. Her hair was choppy and varying lengths, like someone had hacked randomly at her hair until they were satisfied it looked terrible. She'd dyed it a deep purple color to match her toes, but her lighter roots were beginning to show through. She wore makeup, but Olivia suspected she'd had it on for a few days, and it was smudged. She looked up at Olivia and Brock with a dopey smile.

"I don't know you. Or do I? I don't think I do," she said dreamily. Olivia stared at the young girl. She was clearly out of it. She didn't seem like some criminal mastermind who was going around killing people. She simply looked like a teenager stoned out of her mind. But looks could be deceiving of course.

"Are you Pixie?"

"Yes, that's me," Pixie said. She took a drag of the cigarette propped between her fingers. "Who wants to know?"

"We're with the FBI."

Pixie laughed out loud, a husk to her laughter. "For real? Oh man, what've I done this time?"

"We're investigating a murder—"

"Well, la-dee-dah. The stuff I get up to! I'm always being accused of all sorts of crap, you wouldn't believe it. Just because I like to let loose and have a good time. I'll bet that stupid babysitting company sent you, didn't they? They were *so* mad at me when they fired me. Said I'd made an idiot of myself. But it was all temporary, you know? I wasn't going to waste my life working for them. For the *man*."

Olivia and Brock exchanged a look. Pixie was clearly not in the right state of mind for any kind of conversation, but it had Olivia wondering how she was supposed to pull off the crimes they were accusing her of. She didn't even look like she would be capable of tying her own shoelaces—if she in fact had any shoes in the first place—let alone pulling off the perfect murder. Pixie

THE **HOUSEWIFE**

continued to babble to herself, barely paying any mind to Olivia and Brock.

"Sure, I messed around and got in trouble... but all those fancy rich folk had such nice *stuff*! You're telling me that if you were left alone in a mansion you wouldn't sample the champagne and try on all their designer shoes? Because believe me, that was my first thought. That was the only way I was ever getting to wear Louboutins. And yeah, it got out of hand, but so what? No harm was done... They went back to their fancy lives. Kristen said she didn't even *mind*. We were *friends*. It was her stuck-up husband who made a big deal of it."

"Kristen said it was okay for you to have intercourse in her bed while wearing her clothes?" Brock asked, eyebrows raised.

Pixie waved him off.

"Well, *no*, obviously not. But she did let me try on her stuff one time, and I guess I got a little addicted to that feeling. You've never lived until you've worn real fur... oops, I wasn't supposed to admit that. It's fine, the coat was vintage, it's basically vegan! Don't look at me like that... I didn't mean to cause any harm. I was just messing around."

"Pixie... two of your former employers are dead. Kayla and Kristen. Ring any bells?"

Pixie's head snapped up. Her eyes were wide, almost pained. It seemed to have sobered her up a little.

"Kristen? She died?"

"Yes... she died. And she was robbed in the process. And now we're trying to find out why. Did you do it, Pixie? Did your jealousy get the better of you? You said you wanted what they had... Did you steal from them too?"

The fear in her face diffused instantly and she laughed again. "Oh, come on. Really? You think I could kill someone? I'm too high for this, man. Come back tomorrow."

"No, we're talking to you now."

Pixie rolled her eyes. "Alright, fine. Look, I'm no angel. My parents kicked me out when I was sixteen. I messed around in class. I flirted instead of studying. I like to get high. I do things I shouldn't just for the hell of it. I don't like the way this society is built and I don't want to be caged in by it. But I didn't kill anybody. I mean come on, really? I'm not sick like that. Why would I take this life away from anybody, huh? There's so much to do, so little time… I'm not wasting that on hurting people."

"You did hurt people, Pixie. You remember how you let Kristen down?"

Pixie scowled. "I didn't *let her down*. I told her dumb husband, the kid was asleep when I was in her bedroom. And if they had come home an hour later, they never would've caught me anyway. I'd done it, like, three times before that. I know how to clean up a mess…"

"You do realize that sounds bad when we're investigating a murder case, right?"

Pixie groaned. "This is dumb! I didn't do anything like that. You talked to what's-his-name, right? Brad? Brent?"

"Brandon."

"Ugh. I just *knew* he was no fun. I wasted so much time trying to get him to have some fun with me. I shouldn't have bothered. But whatever he's told you, I didn't mean any harm. It was all in good fun. I guess they didn't see the funny side, but I wasn't about to go back and *kill them* over it. God, who would do that? I'm not a murderer, okay? I'm just a girl a bit down on her luck and making mistakes, but that's life, right?"

"So you didn't think to nab things from your employers while you were there?"

"Oh come on. Like they'd let me get away with that. They already kicked me out, I wasn't about to stick around in case they sent the cops after me! Besides, if I was to steal, like, a handbag, what the hell would I do with it then? It's not like I go anywhere fancy enough to need one." Pixie tilted her head back and laughed. "Although, once or twice I did steal a trinket or two… *Shhhhh*, don't tell anyone. They won't miss them."

Olivia felt like putting her head in her hands. So not only was Pixie not their killer, she was also a petty thief who could have easily taken the items missing from the homes of the victims. She was also a totally unreliable source, switching her story every two

THE **HOUSEWIFE**

seconds. Was she a thief or not? She seemed to have forgotten what she was saying as she was saying it.

But if she had stolen anything from Kristen in the past, that meant there was a possibility that the killer wasn't a thief at all—that it had been Pixie doing the stealing all along. That made matters all the more complicated. They'd need to know exactly what Pixie had taken before they could work out if the killer was stealing after all.

Olivia looked at Brock with a pained expression, music thumping around their ears. Brock sighed.

"You keep Pixie occupied... I guess I'm hunting for stolen stuff."

CHAPTER FOURTEEN

Olivia and Brock spent some time in Pixie's home, searching for anything that could connect her to any of the victims. The entire apartment was filthy, and it took some time to get the partygoers to clear out so that Olivia and Brock could take a look around, but even when the apartment was emptied out, their search came up somewhat short.

None of the things that had been reported missing by Brandon showed up. It was a long list of items to check out, and yet it quickly became clear that Pixie hadn't taken anything that had been reported missing. However, Brock did locate a handful of jewelry that had become a tangled mess in a dish beside Pixie's mattress. When Olivia contacted Brandon, he said he recalled that Kristen had lost some a while back.

"Honestly? She had so much stuff that it was hard to keep track," Brandon said. "And I don't care about the stolen stuff. If Pixie didn't kill my wife then she can have everything she owned for all I care. What else am I going to do with it now?"

"I don't think Rebecca would want to hear you say that…"

"Then don't tell her," Brandon said shortly. "Look, if nothing else comes up, just leave Pixie alone. She's messed up enough as it is."

But it was Olivia's job to investigate, and so she pushed on, though she didn't think she would find much else. The whole place was a mess, and the haze of smoke didn't make it any easier to investigate, but Olivia knew they weren't there to make a drug bust. It wasn't like these people had anything to lose anyway. Their drug-fueled lives didn't affect anyone else. For most of them, it was all they had.

But then Pixie told Olivia something that complicated things further. As Olivia was questioning her lying in the bathtub, Pixie began to babble.

"It's not a big deal… I took a few bits and bobs from that rich lady. No one noticed, right?" she said, rolling her eyes. "It was never worth very much. I pawned half of it to get money for some drugs, so I know the value pretty damn well. I should've taken something better. I had my eyes on some of her shoes. Um… why are you looking at me like that?"

Pixie's admission only complicated things even more. If half of her stolen stuff was elsewhere now, then they had no way to know if the missing items Brandon had reported were among the pawned items. Olivia thought it was unlikely, considering it had been a while since Pixie left their employment, but unless she could be certain, they still wouldn't know if their killer was also a thief. Without that key piece of information, it was going to be much harder to build a profile of who they were dealing with.

Eventually, when the day dragged into the night, Olivia and Brock left Pixie's bedside and headed back to their hotel to get some rest. In the morning, they dressed and prepared to go back and investigate more. However, as they were heading out to the car, Brock received a call from the local police.

"We might have a witness," Brock explained as he ended his call. "One of the neighbors of Nell and Karen Young said they saw some things the day of their death."

"They kept that quiet for a while…"

"I suppose hearing that your neighbors have been murdered is enough to loosen anyone's tongue. Let's head over there and see what they have to say. If the information is good, we might finally have something solid to work with."

"I'm hoping so. I don't want to deal with any more unreliable witnesses this week," Olivia muttered bitterly, still thinking about how Pixie had blown the investigation apart with her comments.

They drove straight over to the Young's house and found a middle-aged man with a receding hairline talking to a police officer in front of his home. With his wonky glasses and scruffy clothes, he didn't look like the kind of person to live on such a fancy estate, but his home was just as lavish as the Young's. *Don't judge a book by its cover,* Olivia told herself, walking toward him. She silently hoped that he would be able to offer them something of interest.

The man looked up in interest as Olivia and Brock approached. He smiled at them and turned his back on the officer he was speaking to mid-sentence, eagerly reaching out his hand for Brock to shake.

"Hi. Graham Long. Wow, I can't believe I'm meeting an FBI agent… something to tick off my bucket list, huh?"

"Two FBI agents," Brock said pointedly, nodding to Olivia. Graham didn't seem quite as excited at the prospect of Olivia, but he politely shook her hand, if only to escape Brock's disapproval. It seemed he was eager to get on Brock's good side.

"We heard you might have some evidence to help us out?" Brock pushed Graham further. He nodded enthusiastically.

"Yes. You can consider me an eyewitness… I did see something. I hope it might be relevant. I saw a van arrive on the property the day the Young family were killed. Of course, I

THE HOUSEWIFE

thought nothing of it until I heard that they had been killed... they were always having dinner parties and guests in their home."

"Was this van one you recognized? Did it belong to a company that had visited the house before?" Olivia asked. Graham scratched his chin.

"I don't believe I had seen it before. It was just a plain white van. There was no branding on it or anything, not that I remember. But they must have had permission to come in because there's no getting past the front gate otherwise. You need the code to enter the neighborhood, as I'm sure you saw when you came in today. I guess maybe Nell hired someone to work on the house? Last I spoke to her she'd been hoping to completely redo the kitchen, I think.."

"Did you see who came out of the van? Could you describe the person?"

"I can do you one better," Graham said, his eyes glinting with pride. "I have a security system of my own... and it caught the guests arriving and leaving. Time stamped and all! Come on, I'll show you inside."

"Sorry... Did you say *guests*? Plural?" Brock asked as they followed Graham up to his home, leaving the police officers standing outside. Graham nodded enthusiastically.

"That's right. The video quality isn't the best, I'll be honest... it just catches them in the edge of the camera's eyeline. I guess they parked strategically so they wouldn't be seen. But I got them! There were two people in that van. I couldn't tell you anything else about them... I really wasn't paying much attention. I keep trying to think, but it's hard... It's fuzzy. Like I saw it but I didn't take it in, you know? I never expected something so mundane would become important... but, hopefully, the footage will speak for itself."

Inside Graham's house, he took them through to his living room and offered them a seat. He shifted a laptop onto his knee and began to search through his archives for the camera footage he needed to back up his stories. He hummed to himself as he perused, clearly not reading the mood in the room. Olivia's chest was tight, wanting to know more. All this time, they thought they were looking for one person. If they were looking for a pair, it would make matters much more complicated.

And much more intriguing.

"I hope this will be useful to you… I think you might even be able to make out the license plate of the van if you squint enough. Can I do anything else to help?"

"Maybe let me see a little closer," Brock said, holding his hands out for the laptop. Graham seemed all too happy to hand it over, staring at Brock with a star-struck expression. It wasn't the first time Olivia had seen someone fascinated by them and their work, but Graham was starting to make her a little uncomfortable. He seemed almost too eager to get involved. She turned her attention to the laptop instead so that she didn't have to endure his gaze. Not that he was interested in her anyway—it was clear to her that Brock was the man of the hour in Graham's eyes.

She kept her eyes on the screen. Graham wasn't important, but the security videos were a goldmine. The footage from the day of the murder showed the arrival of a van at around eleven am. As Graham had told them, the van was plain and unmarked with no special features on it. The license plate was also visible, though the grainy image was hard to decipher, considering it was parked at a distance. Still, Olivia hoped that if they paused the video a few times, they'd be able to make out the plate as a whole. That would give them a solid lead on their killer.

Or *killers*.

She was more interested in who was getting out of the van, though. It had occurred to her that two people might be involved in such a complex case—given the amount of legwork they'd need to do to break into the homes, carry out the murders, and then make away with a bunch of stolen stuff. However, now the evidence was undeniable. One of the figures getting out of the car was significantly taller than the other, but otherwise, it was hard to distinguish them. Both of them wore dark colors and their faces were concealed by hoodies. Olivia chewed her lip.

"Interesting that they both chose to cover their faces… even though they'd already disabled the security in the Young household by the time they arrived, according to the timestamps.

That also means they dealt with security before even approaching the property. They came prepared for anything. They don't seem like rookies."

"It's not often we get killers working in pairs," Brock mused. "But they certainly seem like the people we're looking for. Unmarked van, present on the day of the killing, looking like they have something to hide... let's see what time they leave the property."

Brock fast-forwarded the video footage until they saw the two figures returning to the car. The time stamp on the footage let them know that it was at eleven minutes past three. Brock paused the footage to see if anything had changed.

"Over four hours later... They were thorough. They made sure not to leave their mark behind. The killing itself would have been quick... So, then, what were they doing for the rest of that time?"

"They're both carrying bags," Olivia said, pointing at the shapeless sacks that could just about be made out. "Those are almost certainly stolen goods."

"After this, they go back inside again and come back out with more bags," Graham added eagerly, pushing to be involved once again. "I wasn't around when they left, I'd gone for a round of golf so I never saw them leave... but after I heard that my lovely neighbors were dead... I had to watch the footage myself. That's when I called the police in and announced myself as a witness to their arrival. To think, if I'd just stayed home that day... I could've helped them... I might have heard them cry for help..."

"You did the right thing. This is an important lead. And there was almost certainly nothing you could've done. Not without getting hurt yourself," Brock assured him. "Two killers... or one killer, one thief. Items that were stolen were women's luxury goods... same as Kristen's house. Some ornaments, a few handbags, and jewelry. Are we dealing with a man and a woman here, perhaps?"

"A couple, even," Olivia said. "There were multiple stab wounds on each victim... Perhaps they did perform the killings together. But what motivates them to attack women? Two of them were young mothers too... is it purely a financial attack, or is there something more personal here? Some hatred for women who have children?"

"There's any number of things that could make a couple kill in tandem," Brock said. "Maybe they're going after the man's exes... or maybe old friends of the woman that let her down. It could be entirely impersonal... Maybe he's a woman-hater and his partner is all too happy to take down any woman that isn't her. Or maybe *she* is a woman-hater... and he goes along with her to keep her happy. There could be so many different things at play here."

"Well, if we can run the license plate from the van, we might be led straight to them. It seems unlikely, given how careful they've been up until now... but we find that van, and we might have a fuller picture. Zoom in on that to see if we can find it."

Brock spent a few minutes trying to get a clearer view of the license plate. They managed to decipher the first couple of numbers from the pixelated image, but the last few numbers were a little too blurry to make out entirely.

"Is that a zero or an O? And I can't tell if I'm looking at an eight or an S..."

"I don't think we'll get a clearer image than this. We will just have to work with what we have. Run all the combinations and see what we come up with," Olivia said. "We need to work fast... if they've got any sense, they've likely dumped the vehicle by now. But if they haven't then we need to know who it belongs to."

"Then let's get moving," Brock said, standing up. Graham stood too, scuttling after them as they headed for the front door.

"Can I do anything more to help? Do you need me?"

"You've done enough, thank you," Brock said, politely but bluntly, already halfway out of the door.

"It was great to meet you!" Graham called after them as they headed down the driveway. Olivia and Brock exchanged a semi-amused glance. Their job really did bring them across some interesting characters.

But there was no time to chatter about Graham and his strange obsession with Brock. They had several possible plates to look for, and the sooner they located the van, the better.

CHAPTER FIFTEEN

It didn't take Olivia and Brock long to find the van they were looking for, registered at an address three miles away from the property where the Young family lived. It seemed like the only option when they ran the combinations of the license plates that were possible. And when they saw that it was registered as a van, it became clear that they'd found the right one.

Brock drove them as fast as the speed limit would allow, the feeling of time pressing down on their shoulders. Olivia held her breath, wondering if they would get their conclusion to the case so quickly. But something told her that this wouldn't be the end. These murders were meticulously planned, constructed by someone with the brains to pull off such an elaborate operation.

Olivia didn't think for a second that the killer—or killers—would be caught so easily by a license plate. She certainly didn't expect to find the van just sitting, waiting to be found by them.

Olivia wasn't sure what the answer would be—after all, the killers were clearly seen in the vehicle, and there was no denying their suspicious presence—but she hoped they would find out when they got to the registered home of the van.

The address led them to a pleasant, but not overly fancy neighborhood. It was still an obvious far cry from the gated communities they'd visited over the past few days. The people who lived in such an area were not wealthy in the same way, and Olivia could see why a person living there might be pushed to want more. Would someone in a place like this kill for a taste of luxury, to make those better off pay for everything they had? It was possible. And if their killer did in fact live here, then they clearly had delusions of grandeur on their mind.

"This is the one," Brock said as they pulled up in front of the address. Sure enough, the van from the home security footage was sitting on the driveway of the house. Olivia narrowed her eyes on it. It seemed wrong to see it just waiting for them there. Had their meticulous killers been sloppy with their work when they left their van in plain sight? Or was something else at play here?

"The killer didn't even bother to try and dump the vehicle? Something feels off here…"

"Agreed, but we have to check this out. This was the getaway car, after all. Our killers could likely be inside that house."

Olivia nodded. She knew she had to take this seriously, no matter how much the evidence seemed to suggest that something was off about the whole thing. She had to be ready for anything. She checked her gun, nodding to Brock as he did the same. Then they silently got out of the car and walked up to the front door.

Olivia's heart squeezed as they waited for someone to answer the door. They heard footsteps inside and then the door opened, revealing a young man. He had a scraggly ginger beard and bags under his icy eyes. He was a little overweight, the buttons of his shirt straining against his gut. But in his arms, he held a toddler.

THE **HOUSEWIFE**

The child took Olivia by surprise. The young girl had wispy hair the color of her father's beard and her nose was crusted with snot. But she was smiling. Olivia looked between the child and her father. Surely this wasn't their killer? The man going around killing young mothers as he held his own child in his arms? Something about the scene was jarring, considering the reason they were there. It left Olivia without words to say to the confused man on his own doorstep.

"Yes?" the man asked as Olivia and Brock stood before him. "Can I help you?"

"Yes… we're looking for the owner of that vehicle," Brock said, pointing at the van on the driveway. It seemed he was a little thrown off by the man as well. The man sighed, shaking his head.

"Not this again. I've just had the police here about the damn van. It's more trouble than it's worth, honestly. What is it you're so interested in?"

"You tell us," Brock said, raising his eyebrow. The man squinted his eyes, looking mildly irritated.

"I wish I could. It's a mystery to me too. Bought it a few weeks ago for work… just for it to be stolen a few days ago out of the blue."

Olivia's ear pricked up. "Your van was stolen?"

"That's what I said, isn't it?"

"It doesn't look stolen to me," Brock pointed out. "It's right there on your driveway."

"Look, I already told the police what happened… I reported it right away when I found out it was gone. They told me there wasn't much chance of them finding it if I hadn't witnessed the robbery to give them some clues as to what happened. But it turns out they never needed to go looking for it. The thief brought it right back."

Olivia blinked several times. "Sorry?"

"This morning when I got up, I looked out the window and… there it was! Parked back where it had been before. I thought I was seeing things… I've had a few sleepless nights worrying about the whole thing. That van is my livelihood and I wasn't going to be able to afford another. Thought my eyes were playing tricks on me when I saw it outside. But it was right where it is now. Of course I called the police… They laughed me off until they came back and saw it for themselves. What kind of person steals a van just to bring it back? It doesn't make any sense…"

Olivia and Brock exchanged a glance. Olivia turned to the man in the doorway.

"Maybe it does. We're investigating this van in connection with a murder case. The van was spotted on security footage outside a house where the inhabitants were murdered. Two people went into that house and came out with armfuls of stolen goods."

The man gaped at them. "*My van?*"

"That very same van. Then I suppose they cleaned the van and brought it back to you."

The man in the doorway looked horrified. "But… but why would they do that? And why would they pick me out?"

"To give us a red herring to follow," Brock said darkly. "To make sure we spent a little longer off their scent… I guess they picked your van because it's plain and unassuming, difficult to distinguish from others." He shook his head. "We thought the killers were being stupid, but they were one step ahead of us. Again."

"But… but won't there be evidence they were in the car? There's got to be, right? The police have been dusting the van for prints, looking for who might have done this…"

"If the killers have any sense… which they seem to… they will have made sure not to leave a trace behind," Brock said. "But your van was definitely on the scene of the crime. And now we understand why and how." Brock looked up and nodded to the small camera on the outer wall. "Security cameras? You're well prepared."

"Yeah, well, I thought so… I've got some expensive equipment on the property for my business. But the day the van was stolen, my systems were on the fritz. The cameras went out, they didn't see anything at all… as if I didn't have enough to worry about…"

"Sounds about right,' Olivia murmured. She turned to Brock. "I think we need to speak with the police, see if they pulled any evidence off it. If the killers pulled this off once, then it's possible they did this with every murder scene. We should be tracking stolen vehicles, looking for patterns."

"Is there much point? It's only going to slow us down again," Brock said. "The killers won't have left anything behind for us to find. They're far too smart for that. And while we're trying to track the vehicles, the killers will be moving on to their next set of plans…"

"Then we at least need to tell the police what we know and ask them to keep in contact with us. If we can let them handle the stolen vehicles, you never know what they might find."

"Is anyone going to explain to me what the heck is happening?" the bemused man said, but Olivia knew they had no more use for him now.

"Thank you for your time. The police will handle this from here."

"Who even are you? How do you know all this?" the man asked, but Olivia and Brock were already walking away. Olivia's mind was whirring. She knew they were tangled in a complex web with this case, but the more they learned, the less she felt like she knew. As they got back in the car, Brock sighed.

"I suppose you'd better give the police a call and tell them what we've figured out. But then what? Where do we go from here?"

"We keep pushing, like we always do," Olivia said. "It'll take us somewhere eventually. These killers are smart, but that's never stopped us before. I think there must be something we're missing, right beneath our noses…"

"Well if you figure out what it is, you let me know. Because right now, I feel entirely in the dark."

CHAPTER SIXTEEN

IT HAD BEEN A DISAPPOINTING DAY FOR OLIVIA AND BROCK. They'd been so close to answers, and yet so far away at the same time. The wild goose chase had almost left Olivia embarrassed at how easily they'd been lured in by the killer's instincts. She knew that was ridiculous—they had to follow leads as they came up—but they were being played. She could almost feel the killers laughing at them, enjoying how easy it was to make them play to their strings.

Olivia knew days like this were inevitable in her line of work, but it didn't make the whole thing any less frustrating. Cases always consumed her entirely. She lived and breathed them, unable to focus on anything else until the mystery was solved.

THE **HOUSEWIFE**

Coming so close to answers only to be blindsided did nothing to improve her mood.

But her annoyance only spurred her on. She didn't like to back down from a challenge, and she certainly didn't like to believe that there was a criminal out there that could outsmart them. After all, they were professional problem solvers. There had been the occasional criminal who had slipped through her fingers—the Gamemaster among them—but for the most part, she knew how to pin down any and all of the foes she faced. When she didn't, it left her feeling sore, as though she too was being physically attacked by the killers she encountered. And that's what made her want to catch them the most. She wasn't about to let the two slippery thieves and murderers be any different.

They headed back to their hotel room and ate dinner in their room. They'd brought back takeout that was a little cold and disappointing, but Olivia barely noticed. She had one eye on her plate and the other on her notes, attempting to look for gaps in their investigation. They'd been led down several false paths already, but that didn't mean they hadn't been on the right track at some point. If she could work backwards, perhaps she would spot something that she had missed in the heat of a moment. It was often the small things that led to the biggest reveals.

But her thoughts were interrupted by a phone call. She frowned at the caller ID.

Jonathan didn't usually contact them during their cases, often leaving them to their own devices and trusting them to get things done. She suspected that if he was getting in contact, he either had something of value to add to their case…

Or there was trouble on the horizon.

She reached for her phone and accepted the call, pressing it to her ear.

"Hi, Jonathan."

"Knight. Are you alone currently?"

Olivia frowned and glanced at where Brock was polishing off his dinner at the small desk in the hotel room. Why would she need to be alone for a work call?

"No."

"Tanner's with you?"

"Yes, of course."

Jonathan sighed. "Alright... I have some information about the Yara Montague case. And I called you first because I wanted to know if this is a bad time to bring it up to Tanner. I don't want him to be distracted from this current case. I know he's struggled a little with the whole thing, and this case is far too important to have him on edge."

Olivia wavered. There was no way she felt comfortable knowing anything about Yara's case if Brock was being kept in the dark. If he wasn't being told everything, then she didn't want to know either. But on the other hand, she was also concerned about how he might handle news about Yara. As much as he tried to act like he was unbothered by her and everything they'd been through, Olivia knew that he would be hurt if anything had happened to her. There were years of history between them that he was trying desperately to ignore, but couldn't completely let go of.

Olivia continued to waver, but she knew she wasn't capable of keeping this from Brock. He also had more right than any of them to know the truth, even if it did cause him pain. Olivia let out a sigh.

"I don't think it's a good idea to hold this back," she said. "It's sensitive, but we're talking in a professional capacity. I think you need to speak to both of us together."

"Hrm. I thought you might say that. Well, if you're sure... put me on speaker. I'd like to speak to both of you about it now, while the news is fresh."

"Okay," Olivia said. She turned to Brock. "Jonathan would like to speak to us... it's about Yara."

Olivia watched Brock's face, searching for any signs of discomfort or frustration, but he didn't let anything show in his expression. He simply moved to sit beside Olivia on the sofa and she took that as a sign to put Jonathan on speaker. Jonathan cleared his throat.

"You there, Tanner?"

THE **HOUSEWIFE**

"Yep," Brock replied shortly. Olivia knew he must have been listening to the brief conversation she'd had with Jonathan. Perhaps he was irritated that Jonathan didn't trust him with the information in the first place.

"Good. I'm sorry to call about this now, but I figured that I should keep you both in the loop about Yara's case," Jonathan said. Brock scoffed.

"But you weren't sure about whether to tell me at all, were you? You weren't exactly subtle with the way you handled this."

"Brock," Olivia hissed, nudging him. She wanted him to remember that he was talking to his boss, and he wasn't being very respectful about it. But Brock didn't seem to care. Perhaps after everything they'd all been through, there was less need to tread on eggshells.

"If you were interested in *keeping me in the loop* then I suspect I would have been your first port of call. But instead, you went through Olivia."

"I'm looking out for my agent, Tanner. This isn't the time to get snippy about it."

"I'm fine, Jonathan. I'm not made of glass. You think I can't handle the truth?"

"I'm sure you can."

"Then give it to me. I want to know what's going on. Has she been caught?"

Jonathan cleared his throat. "Not exactly. As you know, there has been a team working on tracking her down, and hopefully the Gamemaster simultaneously. They've been working on decoding the message she sent to you about her possible location."

Olivia had thought about the message so many times that she had committed it to memory. *We are at a place that is hidden in plain sight. You could pass us on the street, but you would never see us. Times are tough, but time has become our friend. If you look too hard, you will not find us. If you don't look at all, we'll be right behind you.*

"Our team felt fairly certain that they had decoded the message. Hidden in plain sight… the focus on time… they narrowed it down to a busy location that relates to time…"

"Times Square," Olivia blurted. It had just clicked in her head after months of speculation, after months of hitting a wall. *Times are tough, but time has become our friend.* The location was hiding them in plain sight, keeping them off the radar. They weren't even hiding at all. Olivia pictured the pair of them wandering around the city, anonymous in the crowds. It was risky, but in some ways, it was smart.

"That's what my team deduced, too."

"But they couldn't find her," Brock said. "What a surprise."

Jonathan sighed. "The team went to New York and tried their best to spread out and look for Yara. They hoped they might get it done on the down low and be out before they were noticed. They checked every hotel and empty building, looking for anything out of the usual. But there was no trace of them found. Nothing at all."

"So it was a trap all along," Brock said, rolling his eyes. "What a surprise."

"Not necessarily. The letter you received from Yara is several months old. I think it's likely that they moved on to somewhere else and that Yara hasn't been able to reveal her location again since. Perhaps they moved somewhere that Yara has been kept more in the dark and not give them away. Her more recent letters have been much less detailed, more erratic. Like she wrote them in a hurry."

"So what you're saying is that you're no closer to answers than you were before?" Brock asked. Olivia shot him a look.

"Brock!"

"No, he's right. We're no closer than when we started. And not for lack of trying. You know I've put some of my best agents on this case, but we're still trying to find answers. I'm sorry to bring you bad news, but I thought it was right that we at least approached the subject. The team is going to continue to look into it, but it may well be a dead end."

"And if it is?" Olivia asked. She wasn't sure what that would mean for them, for Brock in particular. He'd handled a lot in the last year, but she worried what it might do to him if Yara never showed up again. Or worse, if she was killed.

THE HOUSEWIFE

"We'll continue pushing to search for Yara and the Gamemaster. They're fugitives from the law, and we have several agencies looking out for them. We're also having to consider the possibility that Yara is dangerous too… After so many months under the Gamemaster's thumb, there's no telling what that could've done to her mental state. It's possible that she's being manipulated so heavily that she could pose a threat. The three of us know exactly what she's capable of, after all. But that's not your concern."

"Not our concern?" Brock choked. "I think it's our concern, don't you Olivia? You made it our concern when you rang to tell us about it."

"I only wanted to make sure you were up to date on your friend, Brock."

"She's not my friend. She proved that much herself," Brock said through gritted teeth. Olivia put a hand on his arm to steady him. She half expected him to pull away, but she felt him relax a little under her touch, his body deflating as he let out a calming sigh. He shook his head, his eyes pained.

"You don't need to update us on this any longer. Like you said, it's not our concern," Brock said. "It's in the hands of the team you picked now. I only want to know when she's finally caught. Okay?"

"I suppose, if that's what you want. I'm sorry again for bringing bad news. I'm hoping that this won't be a distraction from your own work. Am I clear?"

"Crystal," Brock said bluntly. "But if you want my opinion, you're wasting your time looking for them. We'll never find them until they want to be found. The Gamemaster will have prepared for every possible scenario. That's what she's good at—playing life like a game. And when we find her… *if* we find her… no one will be safe. I'm sure of it."

"We'll keep the team advised of your concerns. In the meantime, focus on your current case—and be sure to contact me immediately if you receive more communication from Yara. No more holding back evidence."

There it was—the other shoe that Jonathan had mercifully kept from falling. He was right, of course.

"Of course," Olivia reassured, keeping one eye on Brock in case he had any more outbursts. "We'll make sure to keep in touch."

"Alright. Keep up the good work."

Olivia leaned forward to end the call, but Brock was already standing up and walking back to the desk, his back turned to Olivia. They were silent for a few moments while Brock stared at the wall, his shoulders hunched. Olivia could feel the change of his mood, a dark cloud hanging over his head. She wanted to say something to comfort him, but words didn't feel like enough. How could they be when she knew how dark a place his mind had become? How was she supposed to reach through to him when he was determined to push everyone and everything away?

That was Yara's doing. She had made him untrusting, angry at the world, bitter at his lot in life. Brock had never quite been the same since her betrayal. Olivia's heart felt heavy. It was bad enough that he had suffered betrayal within his own family, but to be betrayed by his friend, a person he chose to have in his life, was another thing entirely. He had done everything to help her—he had risked his life going to the island to save her. And now, she'd left him with nothing but bad memories and a hardened heart.

Olivia slowly stood and moved to him, her hands finding his slumped shoulders and gently coaxing the knots out of his muscles. He allowed her to do it, his posture still hunched like he couldn't bear to hold himself up any longer.

"Tell me what you're thinking," Olivia said softly. Brock let out a long sigh, rubbing at his temple with his fingertips.

"I'm thinking that I almost wish Jonathan hadn't called."

"I'm sorry, Brock... he was debating whether to tell you about it for a reason."

"Because he was being a coward?"

Olivia sighed. "Because he was trying to look out for you. But I understand why this upset you. He didn't handle this well at all. Given the lack of progress, I'm not sure he should've said anything..."

THE **HOUSEWIFE**

"It's fine. It's not his fault, he's doing his job. I know that. I shouldn't have lashed out at him." Brock sighed again, turning to Olivia with pain in his eyes. "I guess I just... Well, I think some part of me just wanted to know if she's okay. If he was going to tell me anything, I wanted it to be some good news. I spend all my spare time just... wondering. I thought if they had a lead on her... then I'd at least know whether she's still alive."

"Oh, Brock..."

Brock pulled away from Olivia, frowning a little. "You don't need to pity me."

"I don't pity you. I'm glad you feel this way."

He barked out a bitter, caustic laugh. "You're glad that I'm distressed by this?"

"Well, no, obviously not. It's not that. I'm just glad that you still care. I thought you had moved past that entirely, that you had nothing left to feel for her. I'm glad you haven't turned your back on her entirely."

Olivia continued to massage his head, his eyes closed.

"The thing is... I have. I condemn everything she did. I don't think there's any reason on Earth that I would do the things that she did. I wouldn't want to betray my morals the way that she did. I know that it's not that simple, that she was coerced, that she was scared. But in her shoes, I firmly believe I would have died before hurting someone else. But... but I don't want her to die. I don't want to know that she died and we couldn't stop it. That we weren't even actively looking for her... letting someone else do it for us. We're all she has left in the world and we haven't even lifted a finger to find her."

"None of this is your fault, Brock. You went to that island to save her. She made her choice to turn on us. And now, it's out of our hands. This isn't our case anymore. You're not supposed to be getting involved, and with good reason. It's too close to home."

"I know... but sometimes I just... I lie awake at night and think of all those letters she sent. The desperation in her words... but I'm always so conflicted. It could easily be a trap. It could easily be the Gamemaster pretending to be Yara to lure us in. We've dealt with enough criminals to know that it's a very real possibility. But it could also be a genuine call for help. My mind just tears itself apart over and over again. We might not be on the island anymore, but the games are still going on in my mind. The Gamemaster has a hold over my thoughts, and it's broken me a little, Olivia."

"Oh, Brock..."

"I tell myself that I should just pull myself together, but it doesn't feel that simple anymore. I trusted her, and she tried to kill me. To kill *you*. After all I've been through in my life... this is the thing that's stuck with me. I don't know what to believe any more, or what to trust, *who* to trust. The only person I trust is you... and what we have together. And I know nothing else should matter, but sometimes, in moments like this, I find myself breathless, out of control. I just want to let go of it all. I want her to be found, one way or another, so that I can end this war inside myself and never have to think about her again. I feel so... weak."

Olivia cupped Brock's cheeks in her hands. "Brock. You're the one that taught me that feeling your emotions in their entirety is not weakness. It's strength. These feelings you feel are controlling you... some people would be floored by them. I don't know how you get out of bed every day when you're facing such complicated emotions. If I was in your shoes, I would've crumbled by now. But you carry on anyway. And the fact that you still have empathy, still have kindness... the island could have made you cold and cruel, but you're still *you*. You're still the man I fell in love with, the man who can make a whole room of people smile, the man who *cares*, even when everything seems to be against you."

"You're just saying that to make me feel better. I'm not the man I was."

"Yes, you are. You're him and so much more. Things have changed, and you have too, but adapting to something so traumatic... that's survival. That's staying strong. I'm proud of you, Brock. You haven't let the Gamemaster win, even if you feel like you're playing a losing game some days. You're still here and fighting for what's right. For as long as you keep that goal in mind, you're always going to win."

THE **HOUSEWIFE**

Brock swallowed, his eyes looking a little misty. He managed a smile, looking up at Olivia with love and care.

"Thank you. For not letting me forget myself. For keeping me in check."

"You don't need me to do that. I'm not your moral compass. You know the way, Brock. You always have."

He nodded slowly, a tear trickling down his cheek. And at that moment, Olivia didn't think she had ever seen him seem so strong. He pulled her onto his lap and they held one another for a long time, clutching one another for comfort. Their lives were an ongoing, never-ending battle. But together, they kept coming back for victory after victory.

And as long as they were together, they couldn't lose.

CHAPTER SEVENTEEN

THE FOLLOWING DAY WHEN OLIVIA AND BROCK WERE called to the morgue to examine the bodies of the victims, there was a quietness that settled over them in the car. The night before had proven to be an emotional one after thoughts of Yara had once again haunted them. Olivia and Brock had spent quite some time talking in soft voices before falling asleep in one another's arms, the weight of the day heavy on their chests.

And now Olivia could feel Brock's discomfort filling the car. He had always struggled to open up to her, preferring to hide his emotions inside his therapy sessions. Olivia knew that he found it easier to admit his issues to someone impartial, someone who wouldn't take on his burdens, someone who was paid to talk to him and not get emotionally involved. Olivia understood his need to keep his emotions separate from his work and from her. He had grown up without support for his emotions, being told to bury them deep in favor of keeping the peace around him. Now, he struggled to connect himself to those feelings and to rely on anyone more than he felt that he should.

But Olivia was more than glad that he had decided to talk to her the night before. Each time they explored difficult emotions, it made her feel so much closer to him. She felt like they had taken a step forward together, and the thought made her feel warm inside. After all, how could they spend a life together if they couldn't communicate the way they had the night before?

But she sensed that he was ready to move on today. It was a new morning and they had work to focus on. The last thing Brock would want was a constant reminder of how he had made himself vulnerable the previous night. It was a new day, and it would bring new challenges. Olivia needed Brock to be sharp for what they had coming in their investigations. And if that meant distracting him from his thoughts, then she was more than happy to oblige.

"Any thoughts on our killer? Or should I say *killers*?" Olivia asked him to break the silence. "I mean, given the scale of the operations they're pulling off, I'm not overly surprised that there are two people involved. Between hacking the security systems, pulling off the murders, and then making off with a bunch of stolen goods, these killers have a lot to get done."

"Not to mention that they're pulling all of it off in the middle of the day," Brock added, the tension in the car ebbing away. "They're smart, for sure. And the way they laid out their red herrings, sending us off in different directions to throw us off the scent… it feels very practiced. I think they've done this before, or at least they've planned for every possibility. They're ready for anything. I still can't believe they hoodwinked us with the van trick."

"We couldn't have known. These guys have taken it to the next level. But what's important is that we learn from this. Not just so that we don't get tricked again, but so that we learn more about our killers. We have to expect the unexpected. That's how we'll eventually get inside their heads."

"Trouble is, everything they do is a surprise to us. We still haven't managed to pin down a motive or how they managed to pull it all off. We don't have a profile of their age, their race, or even their gender, though we can speculate. Usually, we have *something* to go off, but this time, it feels different. Plus, we have a lot of ground still left to cover. We got sidetracked from investigating the employees at the security companies, but I bet that's still a good path to go down. This expertise must have come from somewhere…"

"Agreed. As soon as we're done at the morgue, that should be our priority. However, we still need to figure out what connects security employees to this case… What's the motive?"

"The occupation doesn't need to match the motive, right? It just seems like these killers are using their expertise to their advantage. I'm just not sure as far as motive goes… what kind of people want to kill young mothers and vulnerable women?"

"Women-haters would be a safe bet," Olivia mused. "I mean, we haven't even pinned a gender to the killers yet, but I wouldn't be surprised if they were a couple. A man with a vendetta against women who never gave him what he wanted… and a woman who felt excluded by other women, perhaps? They've got to have a common goal, and that should make them easier to pin down if we can just get into their heads a little. What makes them tick? What puts them on the outside of society, and was that what drew them together? How did they find each other? At what point in the relationship they share, platonic or not, did they decide to become partners in crime? There must be a hell of a lot of trust there, right?"

"Oh, absolutely. If I was a killer, there's no chance in hell that I would trust anyone who wasn't totally besotted with me. There are a few people I can imagine would be willing to take that risk with me. I think you'd fit the ticket, at least…"

"Shut it, mister," Olivia said, trying not to smile.

"Alright, spoilsport. It's true, there's got to be some kind of deep connection between them. If one of them goes down, so does the other, in theory. And their operation only works if they're on each other's side. I think you're right... they could be a couple. Willing to live and die for one another, to take risks, to keep showing up for murder after murder. That's really something. There's not a friend on this planet that I would kill for."

Olivia tried to ignore the elephant in the room. She was certain he had Yara on his mind once again. How could he not, knowing that she had killed to stay alive? Knowing that she might have sacrificed Olivia, or even him, just to cling to her chance at life. Close as he had been to her, there was no way he could've defended her actions. It only made Olivia feel more strongly about her hunch. The relationship between the killers had to be strong, almost unbreakable. And what was stronger than love?

"Given the stolen goods, it's likely safe to assume that there's a woman involved, as well," Olivia continued. "I don't see a man being interested in stealing a bunch of women's handbags and jewelry... they're not likely to know the worth of it in the same way. Not that I know much on the matter, but I know what brands are worth. And while it's not impossible, I don't see any man risking it all for some designer items. What use would he have for them?"

"No, you're right there. It seems more likely that he's stealing those things to keep his partner happy and on his side... materialism at its finest."

"Don't worry. I have no urge to make you steal handbags for me from murder scenes," Olivia said. Brock quirked a smile, his mood lifting ever so slightly.

"We still shouldn't discount the idea that they might be co-workers, or that at least one of them is working for a security company. All the signs keep pointing back in that direction. But that's not going to make it any easier to find them among the masses... we barely have a description to work with, and if the police find nothing in the stolen van, then we won't have any physical evidence either. Something tells me they will have scrubbed that van clean. They will have known exactly the kind of evidence they might leave behind, and I think they did a good job of covering their tracks. They've been thorough at all of the crime scenes, so I imagine it's the same here."

"Yeah, agreed. Well, what other motives could there be? Let's assume we're wrong about the romantic connection between the two criminals. We could still be dealing with two men, at a stretch. They could be two incels, perhaps, looking for some kind of gratification that they're missing. That could explain why they'd be targeting women."

"Potentially though, targeting a lesbian couple feels out of sorts if that's their reasoning. And as far as we know, there has been no sexual element to the killings. Though I suppose we'll find out for sure when we get to the morgue. Speaking of, we're almost there."

Olivia never liked visiting the morgue. Seeing dead people on a cold metal slab, knowing their lives had been violently taken from them, was always a daunting task to face. She knew that as an FBI agent, she was expected to be hardened to things like that, but she was only human. No one wanted to see the things she and Brock had seen. But if it got them answers, then she was eager to speak to the local forensic pathologist, Dr. Robert Whelan. She had spoken with him briefly on the phone, and she was confident that he was more than qualified for the job.

Brock parked them up and they headed inside to meet with him. He was a balding man with a thick black beard and thin lips. His body was thin and wiry, as though he too was among the dead, almost a skeleton. He nodded solemnly to each of them as they met with him, but he made no effort to shake their hands. His hands were red raw from sanitizing them.

"Thank you for coming. I hope it won't be a wasted trip for you… I don't expect I can tell you much that you don't already know, if I'm honest. But let's see. Sometimes there are surprises."

He led them through to a sterile room where Kristen Burke's corpse lay upon a metal table, her body barely covered for her own decency. Her skin had paled in the time she'd been dead, and her body was a mess of bruising and knife holes. Olivia stood at her side, trying not to look at her vacant eyes as she studied the wounds.

THE **HOUSEWIFE**

"I thought that Kristen's body would be enough for the analysis. Too many corpses spoil the broth and all that."

"What a beautiful analogy," Brock said, blinking in surprise. Robert ignored his sarcasm.

"I've made up a file for you with the other victims and their notes, but as far as I can tell, there are few differences in the killings and how they were conducted. I saw no reason to bring them out too," Robert told them. "There's nothing too skillful about the manner in which they were killed... they were all simply stabbed over and over until they died. As I'm sure you know from the scene of the crime, they all lost significant amounts of blood. None of them appear to have suffered any head trauma beforehand, and I found no signs of poisoning or sedating, so it's likely they were conscious when they were attacked. There aren't any significant signs of a struggle... There's some bruising on Kristen's back, so it's possible that she slammed into a piece of furniture in an attempt to escape, or the killer forced her against something... but there's no bruising elsewhere that's out of the ordinary, and the cause of death was certainly the stabbing. Stating the obvious there, really, but I suppose it's always best to clarify."

Olivia frowned. She had been hoping for something more to help them along with the investigation. She'd known all along that the killing was significant mostly because of the set-up it had required, but the bodies they investigated almost always told a story. Surely there was something about the body that was more significant?

"So that's it? No other signs of foul play? Sexual assault, perhaps? We were considering the motives behind the killings and... well, we did wonder, considering that all of the victims are young women."

"No, there was no sign of sexual assault. I understand the conclusion you drew. But the body really is what you see in front of you. I found no traces of bodily fluids, including semen. No hair, no skin, nothing. There's simplicity in this killer's work. In fact, I think the whole process would have been relatively quick for the victims. Each of them was stabbed so many times—upwards of twenty times in each of the cases—so they would have lost blood very quickly. I imagine they suffered, but not for a long period of time. I would hazard a guess that the killer continued to stab them after they were dead."

"That's pretty brutal," Brock said, wrinkling his nose. "Like he was in a frenzied state?"

"That's possible. Or just thorough. Given that there is no skill in stabbing a person the way these women were stabbed, I think they were keen to ensure the death was confirmed."

Olivia hummed. "Maybe it had to do with the thrill of it. But in some other sense, it could just be the thrill of it that persuaded our killer to keep going. The crime itself leans into violence and frenzy. But they never touched her face."

Robert nodded. "In fact, they never touched any of the victim's faces."

"Preserving her beauty, maybe? Some twisted idea of gratification?" Brock wondered.

Olivia shook her head. "Maybe. But there was no sexual element either. I think the killer was possibly trying to find some kind of release… the kind they can't find in everyday life. This killer is chasing the thrill of it… they meticulously planned for some time, and then completed the kills in quick succession. Now, I suspect they'll begin the cycle again. Maybe there's a thrill in the leadup to it all, the obsessive planning… but this killer really gets into the actual act of it, I believe."

"I can't speculate on motivation," Robert said. "That's your job. All I can do is look at the clues the body gives me. But I did find it curious that while the stabbing was so… animalistic, for lack of a better word… there's no evidence left behind afterward. Somehow they're both completely frenzied and completely calculating at the same time."

"Like Dr. Jekyll and Mr. Hyde," Brock mused. "We might be looking at one person who swings back and forth between such extremes. Or, I guess, this could be the work of our second person. In either case, there's an element of planning and calculation that we can't ignore."

"I have to agree," Olivia said with a decisive nod. "If it was just about the stabbing, they could jump anyone in the street, and they could do it more often. But I think there's a sense of them savoring the moment... waiting for hard work to pay off. The killer... or killers... seem intelligent. They must get some sort of buzz off a plan pulled off well. Solving the problem of each obstacle—the security, the schedules these women ran off, the red herrings they planted—it's like they're making a list of ways to succeed in their killings and make the most of them."

"So it's not about the sexual element, it's not about the money, it's not about the women, and in a way it's not even *really* about the stabbings. It's about all of them?" Brock groaned. "And here I was hoping we'd narrow things down today."

"No such luck, I'm afraid," Robert said, glancing down at Kristen's body. "I'll run some more tests and be in contact if I can find anything at all that might help your case."

"Thanks. We appreciate that," said Olivia. "There's got to be something that connects the victims, doesn't there?"

Robert gave a tight smile. "Between you and me, agents, the only way I might be able to help there is with a larger sample size of victims—and obviously, that's something none of us want to happen. If they're as smart as you think they are, they're already planning how to disappear, to escape somewhere else, and do it all over again. Time is not your friend."

Olivia glanced at Brock once again. She saw pain in his eyes—he was thinking of Yara's letter again. *Times are tough, but time has become our friend.* That's what she'd said. Did he feel bitter now, working against the clock when somewhere, Yara and the Gamemaster were getting away with murder, walking away scot-free? Olivia watched Brock's hands clench into fists. His eyes held fury as he locked eyes with Robert.

"Don't worry," he growled. "We'll find them."

CHAPTER EIGHTEEN

BROCK SEEMED TO HAVE A NEWFOUND DETERMINATION IN his work as they left the morgue, hurrying to the car with quiet purpose. Olivia knew they had a long day ahead of them if they were going to get anywhere with their investigations, but she was glad at least that Brock seemed enthused. Brock was never lazy, but there were some days where he really put his all into work. She had a feeling this was going to be one of those days.

As they returned to their base at the hotel, they decided that the best course of action was to follow up on the computers and phones of each of the victims. They also needed to look deeper into the security companies, but it was Sunday, and none of the

THE HOUSEWIFE

companies were open for them to call up. It gave them time to focus on each of the victims individually.

"The call logs might be interesting," Brock said as he took out the devices they'd been given to look through and laid them out on the bed. "If they hired anyone or spoke to someone unusual over the phone, then it might show something that our first glance didn't show up. I'll make sure to check recent voicemails too, see if we can glean anything from those."

"We need to do a deep dive on emails too," Olivia said. "I bet there's something there if we look hard enough. Email inboxes are always a goldmine."

"Let's hope so. We could use a miracle right now."

They started with the call logs. They searched for matching numbers in saved contacts first, but found no matches between the four victims. Olivia wasn't overly surprised, though she was a little disappointed in the fact. Then, they moved on to business numbers and unknown numbers in each of the call logs. Brock's eyes brightened and he nudged Olivia.

"Hey, look. This number is a match with Karla, Nell, and Kristen… looks local, too, given the number…"

"Yeah, I already checked in on that one. I think it's the local hospital, that's what showed up when I searched it online. I don't imagine that's anything out of the ordinary. There's probably only one hospital in this area anyway, and regular visits to the doctor after having kids isn't unusual, is it?"

"Darn it. So close."

"Don't give up. There still could be a match."

But as they continued their search, they couldn't find anything of interest. They went back as far as a year in the call logs and found no other matches. They made notes of the unsaved numbers that they couldn't match to a person or business, theorizing that they might have received calls from different numbers to keep up the killer's anonymity, but Olivia felt like they were clutching at straws with that one. If the killers did, in fact, try to speak to the victims on the phone, then they had no way of recalling those conversations now, and they'd likely have dumped the phones they used anyway. A quick search of voicemails didn't unveil anything of interest either, so they were no closer to finding their killers than they had been before.

"I don't think we're going to get anywhere with the calls," Olivia said. "But let's try the email logs. There's not a single inbox that doesn't have something weird in it. We should be looking for anything from a business of some kind, or from unsaved email addresses."

"We should also be checking the spam, I reckon," Brock said. "If the killer wasn't someone they trust, then emails could have ended up there. And I suppose we should filter opened emails too. The emails only matter if the victims took an interest in them as well."

"Good plan. Let's work on that basis."

"Could take a while…"

"It can take all day for all I care. If it gives us something to work with then it'll be worth it."

It was a lot more fruitful searching through the emails. Right away, they found some matches between the victims and the emails in their inboxes. There were some local companies that had sent them all marketing emails that they'd all opened. Olivia noted down each of them, knowing that if they interacted with any of the employees from the companies, it could have offered them an opening into their homes to provide services, only to end their lives instead. She knew it was likely that most of the matching emails were innocent—after all, they lived in a small area with a limited amount of businesses to interact with— but she also knew that it was possible that one of them wasn't. Their killers were smart and they thought outside the box. If they'd figured out how to use a simple email to trick their victims somehow and lure them in, then they needed to know about it.

It was a while later when Olivia spotted another email of interest. When she glanced across the four laptop screens, she could see that all of them had opened emails from a company in the past few weeks. The company offered a free stay in a local spa hotel in exchange for signing up for a newsletter. Olivia narrowed her eyes at the email. At first glance, there was nothing too suspicious about it. It looked entirely professional, with an email

THE **HOUSEWIFE**

address that looked legitimate, links to a real website, and a well-constructed body to the email itself. But what kind of website asked people to sign up for a newsletter via an email address they already had access to? If they weren't already subscribed to the company, then how were they receiving emails from them?

"Brock, take a look at this. This hotel deal seems a little fishy. I checked up on it... the hotel is real, but there's nothing on the website about a free spa deal. And look, the email it's sent from looks legit, but it doesn't match the one on the website. Neither does the phone number. And when you click the URL in the email, it matches the hotel's website... except for one crucial letter. They faked a lowercase L with the number one. I think it's a fake website used to scam people somehow."

Brock frowned. "Okay... so it's a clever spam email. It's probably a virus or something. It probably downloads something onto the computer when you sign up for the so apparent newsletter."

"Maybe. But all of these women opened the emails and their computers don't seem to be infected. I mean, I've seen virus-infected computers, and these seem absolutely fine. So why direct to a fake website? What if something else happens when you click the link to sign up? What if we're dealing with something smarter?" She chewed her lip. "I want to click on the link."

"Olivia, that's exactly what the spammer wants! Do you have *no* sense of computer safety?"

Olivia hid a smile. "I'm serious. What's the worst that could happen at this point? They're not exactly going to be using these computers again, are they? If it gets a virus, it gets a virus. We can cross that bridge if we come to it. But I'm convinced this is something else. A lot of effort went into this, and whoever sent this email is mimicking a local company. Not some big company that would appeal to anyone... a small, local business. All four of these women had the email, but I'll bet no one else did. They're appealing directly to these four women, and they worked hard to make it look natural. I think there's something more to it."

Brock folded his arms. "Are you sure about this?"

"Well, I've got a hunch. And I always trust my hunches. When have I ever led you astray?"

"Okay… you can click the link if you really must. But if the computer ends up with a virus, you're going to have to call someone to come and fix it. I'm pretty sure you're clueless on how to fix that, aren't you?"

Olivia ignored Brock's jab and clicked on the link in the email on Nell's computer. She watched as a website loaded up. A site identical to the legitimate one uploaded, but Olivia noticed right away that the website address was slightly different. Right away, a popup appeared, prompting the user to input their email address to access the deal. Olivia chewed her lip.

"Looks like the scam is still running. I wonder what happens if we put an email address in…"

"It's like you want to break this computer, Olivia. Leave it alone."

Olivia ignored him again and copied Nell's email address into the system again. When she clicked confirm, she noticed something had changed on the computer. She blinked several times in surprise.

"Brock… did you notice that?"

"Hmm? What?"

"The web camera lights on the computer… it just came on."

Brock stared at the tiny LED that was now glowing above the screen. "Okay, that's weird."

"Or is it? Brock, we're looking for someone who knows their stuff about security. They've managed to hack into a whole bunch of cameras to turn them off in order to pull off the murders. And now we know how they've managed to hack into computers and turn the cameras *on*. The killers found a way to keep surveillance on these women. To get inside their homes before they even set foot in them."

"But what did they stand to gain from watching them on their laptops? It only works for as long as they're in the same room as the computer, or when it's turned on. It's clever, but it's not very effective. Like, if they're trying to get the lay of the land and the layout of the house, it doesn't make much sense."

THE **HOUSEWIFE**

"Maybe it was some kind of perverse way of them watching their prey without them knowing and nothing more... or maybe this is one of the ways they figured out the routines of the victims. We know that they researched the women before each of the kills... maybe it's not as simple as them just being followed around in a public setting. If they had insider knowledge of what goes on inside their homes, then it would make it easier to know how to get them on their own and kill them."

Brock shook his head in disbelief. "Wow. I mean, I was going to say it's a stretch, but our killers have had us on our toes for days. They put in a lot of effort to make this happen."

"They did. I wonder if it worked... Did these women have any clue that they were being watched? Did they notice the camera turn on? And if they did, did they make the connection? Maybe not."

Brock shook his head. "This is why I always cover my laptop camera with tape... I'm far too paranoid to let this happen to me."

They had no reason to be suspicious though, did they? I don't think any of them had a sense they were in danger before they were killed. They were just going about their everyday lives without a care in the world. So maybe they logged in to their computers, saw the deal and thought it seemed legitimate... and it pretty much does. It's just an innocent email to them... if they got this far into it, then I doubt they noticed anything was amiss."

Brock stared into the eye of the camera. Then his eyes widened and he swallowed.

"We should probably switch the computer off. Now."

"Why?"

"If we're right about this, and the killers can see through the camera... that means... the killers might be able to see us now. They might be able to *hear* us."

Olivia's heart squeezed. She hadn't thought that far ahead. She quickly snapped the lid of the computer closed, her skin crawling. She dreaded to think what it would mean for them if the killers knew their faces now, knew that they were investigating the murder cases. Of course, they would know they were being hunted, that the deaths were being investigated, but now they might know that the FBI was involved too. And if so, they also knew exactly who was looking for them. The thought made her mouth turn dry. She just had to hope that the killers had no reason to check the video feeds following the deaths of their victims.

"Well, that was truly disturbing," Brock said, raising an eyebrow. "Now at least we know that our killer is even smarter than we gave them credit for. If they managed to hack all four women, then they had access to their privacy. They could've seen anything… who knows how many schemes they set up to worm their way into the lives of these poor women."

"Imagine what they could do with more time, more imagination," Olivia breathed. "We can't let these people keep going with their schemes… how many other women received that scam email? How many women are they watching right now, just waiting to strike?"

Brock shuddered. "I dread to think. Let's think about this… is there a way we can use this to our advantage? Perhaps we can get someone more tech savvy to try and reverse the video feed and show us our killer's faces… is that possible? Could that work?"

"I don't think cameras work that way, Brock. But if we could get them to trace where the hacking started, that might lead us right to the killers. But that's a little beyond our capabilities. We need to turn the computers over to someone who knows more than we do. And while they're at it, they might be able to get further into the mind of these hackers while we try to search the security companies again."

"It's a plan. Let's get this moving. There's no time to waste."

CHAPTER NINETEEN

E XHAUSTION WAS COMMON IN A CASE, BUT OLIVIA FELT IT in particular at the end of that day. It had been a day of technology that didn't make much sense to her and phone calls to people who knew more about the topic than she did. They had been warned that it could take some time to trace the IP address from which the killers watched the victims, and that it was unlikely to lead them to their killers if they knew what they were doing, but Olivia felt they had to try. After the handoff had been made of the victim's devices, the sun was setting and there wasn't much else to be done. All they could do was wait.

By the time they decided to call it a day, Olivia felt shattered. She lay down on the bed in the hotel, closing her eyes the instant her head hit the pillow. The comfort it gave her was bliss. At least their accommodation was nicer than usual—there were no motels to be found in this expensive little town, so their hotel was small, but relatively fancy, with plush white pillows and a proper restaurant downstairs. They hadn't sampled it yet, but the smell that wafted from the kitchen was incredible. Olivia's stomach rumbled at the thought of food.

"Uh-oh. Looks like we skipped dinner by accident," Brock said. "I must have been in the zone for that to happen... I don't remember the last time I missed a meal by choice."

"I'm happy just to sleep it off," Olivia mumbled into the pillow. "I'm beat."

"Probably because you haven't eaten anything."

"I can't be bothered."

"Hey, Olivia? You know what I was thinking before?"

"How nice it would be just to go to sleep?"

"No... how we didn't celebrate Valentine's Day this year."

Olivia finally opened her eyes and rolled onto her side to look at Brock. "Yeah? I suppose we didn't. It sort of just passed us by. It's not really our kind of thing though, is it?"

"It could be, if you wanted it to be. I can be romantic. I've got moves..."

Olivia rolled her eyes. "I'm not saying you can't. It's just all that commercial stuff that gets me. All the expensive gifts, the pressure to go out and prove that you love one another... I like the sentiment, at its core, but I just think it's a way for corporations to make money out of us. Like everything else in this country."

"Wow. You really sucked the romance out of this thing, didn't you? I'm just trying to say that we should make up for what we missed. Make a date night of it while we're in a nice hotel. What do you say? We could get some dinner, a glass of wine..."

Olivia smiled. "Or we could skip all that and go straight to bed..."

Brock waggled his eyebrows. "I like the way you talk, Olivia Knight..."

"...for a good eight hours of sleep, I mean."

THE **HOUSEWIFE**

Brock made a big show of sighing. "You never let me have any fun. Come on. You're not going to bed until you've eaten something. It's not good for you, and you'll only be hungrier in the morning. We're going to have a big day tomorrow, let's get some food for you."

"I'm too tired to go down to the restaurant…"

"Alright… how's this for a compromise? We order room service, we raid the vending machines, and we end the night with eight hours of sleep. You get what you want and I get something out of it too… you can even put your pajamas on."

"Boy, you spoil me."

Brock frowned. "I was fully prepared to go the whole hog and have a three-course meal downstairs…"

"I'm kidding. It sounds kind of nice. A no frills kind of evening… just what I'm craving. Especially raiding the vending machine… I had my eye on a KitKat earlier."

Brock laughed. "Well, at least you're a cheap date. If we're doing room service, I'm going all out. I'm getting a bottle of their finest red and a lobster thermidor."

Olivia laughed. "I don't think this place is *that* fancy."

"Olivia, do you really think I would get my hopes up without checking first? It's on the menu, and it's coming straight to me. So hurry up and put your order in. I'm starving and you're slowing me down," Brock said, thrusting the menu at Olivia. She smiled as she lay on her back, casually perusing the list.

"You're right. This *is* romantic."

"Olivia, don't make me pick for you. I'm serious. If you don't pick something soon I might waste away."

"So many choices…"

"Olivia!"

She grinned at him, thrusting the menu back at him. "I'll get the chicken in white wine sauce."

"Don't tease me like that. You know I have no sense of humor when it comes to food…"

"And now you're wasting precious time griping about it. Put that order in!"

Forty minutes later, when Olivia had raided the vending machine for soda and candy and Brock was getting antsy for their meal, room service arrived on a gleaming silver tray. Olivia was happily munching away on her KitKat in her pajamas while Brock accepted the lobster thermidor and Olivia's chicken in white wine sauce. There wasn't a table to eat at other than the desk so they propped up their pillows and ate on the bed.

The TV played quietly in the background while they quietly ate off their laps. It was just an ordinary evening in their life, but there was something about it that was making Olivia feel good. Olivia felt warmth filling her up inside. She enjoyed these quiet moments between them. She didn't feel the need for fancy dates or constant conversation anymore, though that had never truly been her style to begin with. They were comfortable as they were. And Olivia liked that Brock respected her wishes. He knew she didn't want to go to dinner, so he'd compromised. He'd known she was tired and so he accommodated. It was the kind of gentlemanly behavior that she appreciated most. She didn't need him to fight in her corner, to defend her honor, or save her from harm. She just needed him to respect her and have her back.

And she thought, deep down, he'd known this was so much better than celebrating actual Valentine's Day together. She was sure she'd made her feelings about the holiday clear before, and now she knew that he'd listened to her. She wondered if it was deliberate, the way he'd treated the holiday like any other day without making a fuss, only to acknowledge it later in a way that she would appreciate. He really was a perfect guy, in her eyes. She found it so much more romantic to enjoy his company on any other given day, knowing that a day of love meant nothing if the rest were dull and lifeless. She liked that today, they were choosing to show love to one another, without the fuss, without the fanfare.

It made her heart swell.

She glanced over at Brock, who was finishing up his dinner, smiling to himself. How could she not love that face of his? When he was smiling, it made something inside her lift, like she was floating on clouds. She had a sudden urge to touch him. Her hand reached out to rub his back gently. He turned to her and his smile grew even more. That made Olivia's heart squeeze. No one had ever looked at her that way until Brock came along. No one was ever so pleased to have her around. She knew her flaws—she was obsessed with work, she took life too seriously sometimes, she had long been an emotional wreck. But Brock had come along and wiped the slate clean for her. He had reminded her that there was more to life than work. He had shown her the fun in life again, and brought out the easy-going side of her that she'd buried deep. He never tried to tell her to walk away from her trauma—he helped her embrace it. Because there was more to the eye with Brock. On the surface, he was the funny, food-loving man who didn't take anything seriously. He was the sort of guy women sought out for his good looks and his charm. But beneath that, he had so much more to give.

And he gave her it all and more.

"You good?" he asked her, sensing her mood shifting. She smiled back.

"Yeah. Really good, actually. Thank you for tonight."

"Is this the kind of romance you were looking for?"

"I guess it was. And I didn't even know it."

He grinned, putting his tray of food on the floor and grabbing her by her waist. "Come here, you."

She giggled as he pulled her close to him, her back against his chest. He nuzzled into her neck and pressed a gentle kiss there that had Olivia shivering in delight.

"Still tired?" Brock asked her, threading his fingers through hers. She blushed.

"Kinda. But I also don't want to go to sleep just yet."

Brock kissed her neck again gently. "Me neither. There's something in the air tonight, Olivia. Or maybe it's the exhaustion making things a little cloudy... but I feel close to you."

Olivia squeezed his hand. "I feel the same... sometimes I have moments like this and I just think... What if this was forever? And it makes me feel good to imagine it."

"Yeah?" Brock murmured, his breath hot on her skin. "I think I like the sound of forever with you, Olivia Knight."

Olivia turned to face Brock, feeling a little breathless. What was he implying? Was it what she thought it was? Her heart beat fast, imagining how her life might be about to change forever. He smiled, pulling her in for a gentle kiss.

"But when I ask you to marry me, it won't be mid-case in a hotel when you're half-asleep," he told her. He grinned. "And I'm going to need you to promise you'll say yes before I start thinking up a proposal."

Olivia laughed a little breathlessly, almost relieved that it wouldn't be happening right there, right then. She wasn't sure her heart could take it yet.

"Well, I can't make any promises. There's always time for a knight on a white horse to come in and sweep me away…"

"Over my dead body," Brock said wolfishly. "And I mean that literally. No one else is having you while I'm alive."

"Ditto," Olivia said, brushing her lips against Brock's again. There was an electrical charge still lingering in the air, making her feel alive. Would it always be this way? She couldn't imagine it any differently. The world just changed when she and Brock were alone together, in the best possible way. She kissed him again and he held her close, their bodies pressing together. She gripped the back of his shirt in a fistful, needing him closer to her.

She supposed sleep could wait a little longer.

CHAPTER TWENTY

It was back to business for Olivia and Brock the following day. After a romantic evening spent together, Olivia's heart felt lighter, but her head was entirely in the game. It felt like they were finally getting somewhere with their investigations, like they could maybe push through to get to the truth. They might have been pulled from side to side, turning down the wrong path so many times, but as they returned to investigating employees at local security companies, Olivia felt sure they were onto something.

Because how was it possible that any ordinary person could come along and pull off what their killers had? Hacking the cameras in the victim's computers only proved further how advanced their tactics were. Olivia had seen a lot during her career, but she had never encountered something so calculated and complex. It didn't help that she didn't know much about computers and hacking. They had handed the computers over to the lab experts who could figure out what their killers were up to quicker than they could, so it was time to focus on the local security branches. Now, if they could only get a few suspects, a few names of their potential killers, they might be able to match it up to the evidence on the computers and have solid evidence against their clever opponents.

Olivia was deep into her search for ex-employees now. The current employees in all of the security companies seemed clean, especially given that most of them were loyal to the companies they worked for. None of them had hopped between all three companies, and only a handful had worked for more than one of them. Olivia was sure that they were looking for someone that connected all three of the companies together, given that the hacker had known how to take down the three types of security systems. Sure, anyone smart enough would probably be able to take them all down without an issue, but Olivia knew it would be a lot easier if the killers knew what they were dealing with before going in. Perhaps it was even how they chose their victims, selecting them from customers of each of the companies so as not to form a pattern. That would explain why they were finding it so hard to pin them down.

Fortunately for Olivia, it was her job to look for patterns where no one else would. If the killers were actively avoiding leaving a trail, that was a pattern in itself. She just had to keep following the trail far enough to get her to the killer.

"I've got my list of ex-employees now," Olivia said. "I'm thinking I'll try and do a deeper dive on them all as much as possible. Criminal backgrounds, social media presence, yada-yada. There isn't a huge list to get through, so I bet I can get answers today if we're really lucky."

"Well, I hope something comes up, because I'm stumped. I don't see any current employees with a history at any other companies, and they're certainly not coming up on the system as troublemakers. None of them have got in trouble or had any

THE **HOUSEWIFE**

warnings at work... there's one with a parking ticket from a few months back, but that's not the kind of crime that escalates to murder, is it? They seem like a huge bunch of nerdy rule-followers, based on their profiles."

Olivia rolled her eyes. "*I'm* a nerdy rule-follower, Brock."

"Yeah, but you're cute," he quipped right back. "And you're way more interesting than some of these guys..."

"Never judge a book by its cover, Brock."

"I would agree if I thought it applied here. I know nerds when I see them. They're a lot easier to identify than murderers, and the two rarely cross paths," Brock said with a yawn. "I'll go and grab us some coffee. See what you can come up with."

"I'm good for nothing until the coffee gets here, but I'll certainly try."

Olivia rubbed her eyes as Brock left the hotel room. They were starting to ache after a long time staring at a screen, but she wasn't ready to give up just yet. She was sure she was on to something. Her gaze was a little fuzzy from rubbing her eyes, but she pushed herself to keep at it. The case wasn't going to solve itself.

She made her way through the ex-employees list, starting with the ones who had worked at two or more of the companies. Ideally, she was looking for someone who had been hired by all three, but she was willing to keep her mind open. She had it in her head that she might be looking for a bitter ex-employee, someone who had a reason to throw the security businesses under the bus. She imagined that it could be a competitive business, and one that didn't tolerate mistakes. But then again, their killers hadn't made a single mistake yet, so it didn't seem like they were looking for someone who had been fired for messing up. No, she thought it was more likely that she was searching for someone who had been let go for bad behavior. And if they *had* been fired for something, they must have done something inappropriate. Whatever that was, it might indicate the killer to them. She came across four employees who were of particular interest to her.

"Corey Fulton, Danny Henderson, Matt Stevens, and Terrence Campbell," Olivia murmured aloud. "All of them worked for at least two of the companies at some point... none of them lasted more than a year in their postings, which is a pretty high turnover. Three of them were fired. Corey Fulton is the only one that left on his own accord."

She drew up three separate searches for the men in question. She left Corey out, not sure that he fit her profile. She would return to him as a last resort, but she had a good feeling about the other three. She continued to murmur to herself as she investigated.

"Now, their LinkedIn profiles and social media indicate that they've moved out of the security business or gone solo... Terrence Campbell seems to be doing pretty well for himself. He's got a lot to put on the line if he is the killer... "

She moved on from Terrence. She pulled up Matt Stevens's social media and blinked in surprise. In one of his pictures, he had his arm around another man who looked startlingly similar to him, though a little younger.

"A brother," she murmured. They *had* been looking for a pair. Their main speculation was that they were looking for a couple, a man and a woman, but they hadn't ruled anything out. Now, there were two brothers in front of her eyes, both who fit their profiles. She hummed to herself.

"I wonder..."

She scrolled further through the profile, searching for family members who might be a match, but the last name didn't bring up any matches that looked like the brother. She suspected one of them must have changed their name for some reason. When she realized it would be a slow process scrolling for a face she knew, she instead decided to search up the connecting names on his friend's list.

"Corey Fulton... not a match," she said. There was no Corey within Matt's friend list. But as she was typing Danny Henderson into the search bar, it immediately came up with a match. Sure enough, when she clicked on Danny's profile, she saw Matt's brother looking back at her. He was the spitting image, though he had a cocky smile playing on his lips and he stood alone in his photo. His profile indicated that he was married, though it didn't say to whom. He had over a thousand friends on the app, and he exuded the kind of confidence that Olivia was sure they were searching for in their killers.

Was this them? Was this their double act?

She sat back in her chair, her mind whirring. Everything seemed to fit, but she needed proof. She needed more.

And she was determined that she would get it.

Brock returned with two steaming mugs in hand.

"They didn't have any milk at the coffee machine… so your cappuccino is looking a little sad."

"Never mind that," Olivia said impatiently. "I think I might have a lead."

She ushered Brock over to look at what she had found. She showed him the two profiles of the young men, pausing a little longer on Danny's profile.

"Two employees that worked short term for two of the companies we're investigating, And they're brothers," Olivia said. "They seem close, given that Matt has his brother on his profile. We're looking for a duo, right? They've got the background, they've got the means. They live locally, too. We could be on to something here."

"Were either of them fired?"

"Both of them were from their most recent employer. But they both left postings at other places pretty fast too. They couldn't seem to hold the jobs down, either way. Matt now runs his own security company. It's small, but it seems to be holding its own. I guess it gives him more leeway, more anonymity if he's targeting the clients and no one has heard of his business."

"Okay… but none of the victims used his services, right?"

"Right. But between the two of them, they worked for all three companies. That's why we couldn't find someone who worked for all three. And if they joined forces…"

"So we're not working with the assumption of a woman and a man working together anymore? I know we said we'd look at other options, but what about all the stolen goods?"

"I know, I know. But this can't be overlooked. Look, I know it's not a perfect match for what we've been looking for. But this is a close match, and it opens us up to other possibilities we hadn't considered before. There are two others that could fit our criteria... but none of them have a family match like Matt and Danny, and they don't have connections with the other ex-employees to make me think they were a team. These two have possible motives and means. We can't pass up the chance of looking into them."

Brock nodded. "Okay, you're right. It's worth looking into. How do you want to play this?'
"I think we should go straight to Matt. Look, he's got his home address as his business address. We can go right there, try and talk to him. If he runs scared, we will know he's got a guilty conscience."

"That doesn't seem smart, having that information readily available online… Are you sure this is our guy? I had it in my head that our suspect would be a little smarter than that."

"Maybe he's just cocky. Maybe he has no idea we're on his scent."

"If he's innocent, then no, I doubt he's expecting FBI agents to show up at his door suspecting him of murder."

Olivia shot Brock a look. "If it's a bust, it's a bust. But I think we have to at least talk to him. We've got nothing else. What do you think?"

Brock shrugs. "Alright. I trust you. We haven't got anything stronger to work with. Let's do this thing."

CHAPTER TWENTY-ONE

Matt Stevens's house was on the outer edge of town, and was certainly not a fancy place. After driving through rich neighborhoods with pristine pavements and neatly lined hedgerows, it was a slight culture shock to enter his neighborhood. The other houses were simple, but well looked after, but the same could not be said for Matt's address.

When Olivia and Brock pulled up outside, they could see that the house had fallen into disrepair. The front lawn hadn't been mowed in some time and there was a pile of beer cans stacked up by the recycling bin. Some of them had spilled over onto the grass, and another rattled toward the pavement and then crunched beneath Brock's wheels. Olivia felt her first stab of uncertainty.

Was their killer really living in such squalor, given how prolific they seemed to be?

There was no car on the driveway, but there were lights on inside the house indicating that somebody might be home. Olivia spied a small TV playing inside, and someone clearly was sitting in front of it in the darkness. Nothing about the home screamed wealth or prosperity. From the state of the place, it almost felt like it was housing someone who was down on their luck, someone who had given up on themselves and their life. It wasn't what Olivia had imagined from their killer.

"So much for the home of a mastermind," Brock muttered. Olivia shrugged as she readied herself to go up to the house.

"It could be a front. Everything else about our killers has been so far. There's been too many mind games to know what about these people is real. Besides… This is the best lead that we have, and it looks like the suspect is home. I say we just go up there and ask some questions. If he feels backed into a corner, he might tell us more than he would usually. Or he'll leg it and we'll know he's got something to hide."

"I guess we're going to have to rely on that. I don't know how else we would get him talking. Especially if he's not involved at all."

"I've got a feeling about this. Have I ever been wrong before?"

"There's always a first time," Brock said, but there was a teasing glint in his eye. Olivia sighed. She knew he wasn't taking the lead as seriously as she was. There were a lot of assumptions in the conclusions she had drawn. But if making some wild suggestions got them closer to the truth, then she wasn't about to back down now. The worst that could happen was that she could be wrong.

She wasn't often wrong.

Olivia and Brock made their way up toward the house. Olivia could hear the buzz of the TV inside, low and dull. Otherwise, the place was silent, almost as though nothing had ever lived or breathed inside the house. Olivia felt a flicker of nerves, but she wasn't about to back down now. She took a deep breath and knocked on the door. They were only there to ask questions, but she felt better knowing she had her gun at hand should she need it. If they really were about to come face to face with their killer,

THE **HOUSEWIFE**

then they needed to be ready for anything. They were dealing with a person—or duo—that had gotten away with four murders, and likely more out of town.

They couldn't assume that they were safe.

At first, nobody came to the door. Olivia knocked again, louder this time, and waited. She thought she heard a sigh as someone approached the door. There wasn't much urgency to the gesture. The man took a while fiddling with various locks before the old door creeped open.

The man in front of her was clearly Matt Stevens—the same man she had seen on the social media profile—but the time since the photo had been taken had not been kind to him. It was clear to Olivia now that the photo must be at least a few years old. Matt's body had filled out and his belly strained against the fabric of scruffy gray joggers. There were crumbs covering his old band t-shirt and his facial hair was unkempt. Olivia was soon affronted with a smell of body odor and beer. Matt eyed Olivia and Brock lazily, not registering the guns on their belts or the badges they presented. It was almost as if he was sleepwalking, barely present though he stood before them. Olivia thought of the pile of beer cans and wondered if that might've been the cause of his current state.

"What are you doing on my property?" Matt grumbled, his voice rough like he'd been smoking a lot. Judging by the smell of him and the smog inside his house, he had.

"You're Matt Stevens?" Olivia asked, keeping eye contact with the man before her. She wanted him to know he was dealing with someone serious. He looked back, blinking blandly in disinterest.

"Who wants to know?"

"Agents Knight and Tanner with the FBI. We are here investigating a number of crimes that have occurred—"

The door slammed in her face. Olivia glanced at Brock. Was he for real? She turned back to the door and then knocked again.

"We're going to need you to come back out, Mr. Stevens," Olivia called out.

"I don't want to talk to you!"

"I'm afraid this isn't negotiable, sir," Brock said. "We might as well tell you the full truth of the matter. We have reason to believe the person we're looking for in a string of murders has a background in security and could have been fired from their job... sound familiar?"

"You don't know what you're talking about," Matt snapped from the other side of the door. "Look, my life might have gone down the drain, but whatever it is you're accusing me of, I have nothing to do with it. I spend my days here waiting for a miracle to pull me out of this black hole I've fallen into. I had to sell my car, my computer, and half my other stuff... I've been kicked into the dirt already. I don't need you making it worse by accusing me of... what did you say? Murder? The only thing that I've killed is my reputation. Now you're here trying to make it worse."

"We're not trying to kick you while you're down," Olivia said. "We're trying to figure out why bad things keep happening to women in this town. All of our leads have brought us here. You say you didn't do anything, so explain yourself. If you're innocent then you've got nothing to hide. Come back out and speak to us. I won't ask again."

There was a long pause, and Olivia thought she was going to have to come up with some other method of getting inside, but then slowly, Matt reopened the door. His eyes shifted between Olivia and Brock, guilt written all over his face. Then, eventually, he stepped back to let them inside. Olivia nodded respectfully to him.

"Thank you. We just have some questions. Then if everything adds up, you'll never have to see us again. Okay?"

"Fine," Matt said tightly. Olivia was hit by the smoky air as she walked through to the living room. It tickled the back of her throat and made her want to cough, but she held back, not wanting to seem passive-aggressive when they finally had him on their side. She could see how sparse the room had become, and Olivia wondered just how much Matt had to sell in order to be able to stay in his home. There was no sofa, just one armchair that was covered in blankets to hide how scuffed it was. Matt looked ashamed as he gestured to the room.

THE **HOUSEWIFE**

"Sorry about this place. Not that you're here for that. I don't get too many guests these days... it doesn't matter if it's an absolute hole when it's just me here."

"You said... you said you had to sell a lot of your belongings," Olivia said carefully. "Why? What happened? We know that you worked for a couple different security companies in town, but that you didn't stay long at any of them."

Matt scoffed sourly. "I don't know what the hell you've heard about me, but I wasn't always like this. I was up and coming in my field. I was doing well for myself. I worked for Stronghold first, but that was almost a stepping stone in my career. I knew the other companies would pay better once I had experience, so I hopped jobs after a year because I got a job offer from Fortress. They're the best in town, and they pay a hell of a lot more than the others did. So if it looks like I moved through companies quickly, it wasn't because I was forced to. I chose to aim for Fortress. But the thing is, they're pretty strict there, and they don't tolerate bad behavior or mistakes." Matt ran a hand through his thinning hair. "And that's what screwed me over."

Olivia frowned. "What did you do?"

Matt's eyes flashed with annoyance. "*I* didn't do anything. The issue with the job had nothing to do with me. The trouble started later. That was when my brother also worked there. Danny was... well, he always has been... trouble."

Olivia and Brock traded a look. "What kind of trouble?"

He sighed. "Ever since he was a kid he's been getting himself into messes. He loves to push the boundaries and every button he can. Nothing can keep him in line. Not even me. I've always tried to stick up for him. He's my brother, you know? Our parents didn't even want anything to do with him after a certain point and his life was sort of going down the drain... so I helped him get the job at Fortress. The thing is, he sold himself pretty well. He's a genius, really smart, really capable. He really knows his stuff when it comes to security. Of course, they wanted to hire him. But, that's when the issues started for me... he's never figured out how to conduct himself, how to make a good impression and make it last. Probably because at his core, he's a piece of work."

Olivia glanced at Brock. The more she was hearing about Matt's brother, the more he sounded like he could be the person they were looking for. A genius troublemaker who was savvy with security and had trouble fitting in socially? He fit the bill entirely.

"Tell us about the day you were fired," Brock said gently.

Matt shifted and lit up a cigarette despite Olivia's protestations. "I was called into the office one day at work... Danny was already there. I knew something was up. This was maybe two, two and a half years ago now... I felt like a parent being called into school to deal with my kid. The boss sat me down and told me that he'd caught Danny doing something... something despicable... "

"What was it, Matt?" Olivia pushed gently. He swallowed, his throat bobbing.

"After he'd installed some of the security systems in people's homes... he was hacking into them and capturing... raunchy videos. Don't ask me why because I wouldn't know what to tell you, but a lot of these rich clients install cameras in their living rooms and bedrooms. Whatever makes them feel safe. At least if something happens, there's evidence, I guess. There was one couple in particular that were affected. They had cameras everywhere in their home, and Danny had installed a backdoor into their system. He could remotely access all their feeds on his personal computer. And he kept catching them in the act... all over the house. I don't know why he wanted to do it... I keep telling myself he's not a pervert, that he only did it for a laugh, but it got worse from there. It turned out he was making money off those videos... he was uploading them to porn sites. That's how the couple found out, incidentally... I think they were more miffed that he was making money off them than the invasion of their privacy. Seems like they had similar goals in mind. Anyway, they figured out what had happened and reported it back to Fortress."

"But... but if it was your brother that did it, then why was that your problem?" Brock asked. Matt let out a weary sigh, his body deflating.

"He tainted me by proxy. No one wants to hire the pervert's brother, right? I didn't help myself... I'd vouched for him, and

THE **HOUSEWIFE**

always tried to talk my bosses down when he'd got into more minor incidents. Turns out that just sealed my fate. If he was going down, he was sure as hell going to drag me down with him. I tried to read up on my rights, to see if I could sue the company for firing me in association with my brother... but in the end, I didn't get anywhere with it. I'd just bought my house, thinking I had a job for life, and I couldn't afford a lawyer. So I just sort of accepted my fate. I sold pretty much everything. I live off rice and beans. I barely make enough remotely to not be homeless. And now I'm just trying to get out of the hole."

"That's completely wrong. I'm sorry that happened to you," Brock said. Matt let out a heavy sigh.

"Yeah, well, it sucked. But staying at that job would've been hell anyway. All my friends at the company turned on me. They thought Danny was some kind of weirdo... and they didn't want to know me after that. I tried to go back to my old job, but my record was tarnished and I had no reference from Stronghold. They were still mad that I ditched them in the first place. I told myself that I wasn't the problem. For a while, I was in pretty deep denial. I tried to convince myself that Danny wasn't an issue... that it was just a prank gone wrong, that he was good, somewhere deep down. But after a while, I couldn't even bear to think about him anymore. I cut ties with him over a year ago. He kept trying to get me to talk to him... he used to come by the house and I'd have to lock the doors to keep him out, pretend I wasn't home..."

"So you haven't spoken to him in over a year?"

Matt shook his head, his eyes full of pain. "I couldn't do it anymore. I'm the only one who has stuck by him all these years... I was tired of him ruining my life as well as his own. I always wanted to see good in him, but I guess it never really existed. I was living a delusion."

Brock gave him a sympathetic look. "I know what that's like."

Olivia cut a glance at him. Was that really how he felt about Yara? She didn't want to believe it.

"And now I'm free of him, but it's too late for me. No one will hire me. I set up my own business, but people talk. It's hard to build a new reputation on your own when no one wants to vouch for you, and this isn't a big town. And meanwhile, I'm sure that Danny is doing fine. He didn't end up doing jail time for any of it… he came to a settlement with the couple he harassed and paid them a large sum to get off scot-free. God knows how he wrangled the money. He got a job over at Techtite and he and his wife are still together, as far as I know. Though they always had a rocky relationship. I know firsthand that having any kind of relationship with my brother is near impossible. I think he was cheating on her for a while. I overheard them arguing about his 'side piece' one time. Maybe he's gone off with her. At this point, I can't find it in myself to care."

The more Olivia learned, the more she was certain that Danny Henderson fit the profile of who she was looking for. But from the way Matt spoke, she didn't believe he was the partner in crime. He could be a good actor, but there was no faking the way he lived, the clear decline in his physical and mental health. He looked like he hadn't slept in weeks, worry lines forming on his face and giving him premature wrinkles. He seemed miserable, but there wasn't a bitterness to him like she expected. For someone who hadn't had much luck in life lately, he seemed like a decent person. She couldn't see him going into a partnership with the man who had ruined his life, especially not to go on a murdering spree. Besides, judging by Matt's home, he wasn't stealing expensive things from rich dead women. He could barely afford to feed himself. One designer handbag would pay his mortgage for a month, but instead, he was selling his furniture to stay afloat.

That left just Danny. Olivia needed to know if he was relevant. After all Matt had revealed about him, he clearly wasn't a good man.

But was he a killer?

"Matt… we need to know more about your brother. We're investigating four murders in the local area. Someone hacked into their security systems and watched them, learning their routines… and then killed them," Brock said. "We came to you because we were looking for someone who had worked at all three of the companies we've discussed here today. But everything you've told us about your brother... he sounds like he could be the one we're looking for."

Matt nodded slowly. "I guess I learned, slowly, that he's just not a good person. It was hard, but I'm coming to accept it now. He's no brother of mine. We're nothing alike."

"Do you think Danny would be capable of hurting people? Do you think he could go that far astray? I know that's a difficult question to answer... but we need an honest assessment."

Matt wavered. Olivia could see there was still a shred of care inside him for his brother. The same sort of care that Brock still harbored for Yara. He didn't want to throw his sibling under the bus, even after all they'd been through. But when Matt hung his head, Olivia knew what his answer would be.

"I think... I think he has a violent streak inside him. I was never on the receiving end of it... I think I was the only person he ever truly cared about. As far as I went, he always held back. But I saw glimpses of it. He used to trash my parent's house, throw things at them, kick and scream at them... but only ever behind closed doors. In public, he always seemed like a good kid. He had everyone thinking that my parents were crazy for accusing him of those things. But he's a master manipulator. How else could he get away with the things he has? As for murder... God, I don't even want to entertain the idea. But I... I think it could be something he'd be capable of, if he really let loose. If he let his inhibitions take hold." Matt shook his head, tears squeezing from his eyes. "I feel like I'm betraying him... I know that's crazy, after what he did to me, to my life... but we grew up together. He's always been in my life... I don't want to condemn him. Especially if I'm not sure."

"Think of the women he could have hurt," Brock said gently, putting a hand on Matt's arm. "They only get justice if we find who killed them. Even that is barely enough. It doesn't bring them back, after all. But their families deserve the truth. They were young, they had exciting lives ahead of them... all of that's over now. I suspect you're not the only one who had their life ruined by your brother, Matt. Help us get to the bottom of this. Help us make this right."

Matt wavered, his lip wobbling a little. Then he nodded, sniffing to himself.

"Okay. What is it you need me to do?"

Olivia looked to Brock for an answer. They hadn't thought this far ahead. They needed to make contact with Danny, to try and get him talking. But if he was the killer they were looking for, he would be suspicious of new faces, unwilling to speak to them. Not to mention that if he'd caught sight of them in Kristen's webcam, there was no way they could approach him.

No, they had to try some other method of contact, to trap him in a vulnerable moment where he was likely to be honest. If there was anyone he was likely to trust, it was his brother. But Danny seemed too clever to be caught by a ruse. They would have to get Matt to contact him and make it seem genuine. That was the only way they were going to catch Danny slipping up.

"We're going to need you, Matt," Brock said, voicing Olivia's exact thoughts. "You'll need to put on a good show. Call him up for us. Make your brother believe that you want to be back in his life. Then keep him talking and see what you can glean from the conversation. But I suspect he'll be suspicious, given the timing. If he truly is a wanted man, he's not going to open up so easily. You getting back in touch after he's possibly carried out four murders? He could see through that, if he's not feeling sentimental. He might already know we're on to him."

"Do you think… Do you think it could be dangerous? To contact him?" Matt asked. "For me, I mean?"

"We need to know what's going on in that man's head. We'll keep you safe if it comes down to that. But first, we're going to need you to poke the bear."

CHAPTER TWENTY-TWO

"**R**EMIND ME WHAT EXACTLY YOU NEED ME TO DO? What should I say?" Matt asked as he stood with his phone in his hand. He was sweating a lot, dark circles forming under his armpits and his forehead glistening. Olivia knew that what they needed from him was a big ask—they were asking him to essentially betray his one and only brother—but it was an absolute necessity. From what Matt had told them, he might be the only person that Danny trusted. If he was their killer, then they needed to get him talking and hopefully loosen his lips.

Before Danny figured out that they were on to him.

"We just need you to keep him talking on the phone. Ask him about how he's been maybe, see if you can imply that you'd like to make amends to your relationship," Brock prompted. "If you can try and arrange to meet up, even better. A face-to-face would be super useful to us. The closer you can get to him, the more likely it is we can get a true picture of what he's up to and what he's thinking about."

"And you're just going to stand and listen?"

"We need to try and see his state of mind, try and build a picture of what he's like as a person," Olivia said. "And we can't risk coming into contact with him until we know more. It might sound strange, but even just hearing him talk will be really useful to us. It's about gaining knowledge of him without tipping him off to our suspicions." She paused, her expression softening. "I know this is going to be difficult for you, Matt, but it could be crucial to saving more lives."

"I second that. Four women are dead already. If your brother is involved, then we need to know," Brock said, more firmly than Olivia.

Matt nodded shakily. "I get it. I do. It's just… Well, he's my brother. We grew up together. And despite everything… Well, I still love him. Even if he's a… a killer."

"Try to think of it this way… if your brother is behind this then he has a sickness. A sickness that can't be cured out in the real world," Brock told him. "And the longer he's out here, the more people will suffer from his sickness. Or at least, they'll be on the receiving end of it. He doesn't belong in the real world, walking among innocent people who could get hurt by him. You already know that though, don't you? He's always been different. He's always struggled to cope with ordinary life."

Matt nodded slowly, looking guilty. As though somehow it was his fault his brother had turned out so badly. Brock clapped a hand onto Matt's shoulder.

"I can see that you're worried. Let me tell you something that might help you along… I have a friend—one of my closest old friends, actually—who has done bad things. Terrible things. She killed a person. She worked with a high-level criminal to save her own skin. She kidnapped Olivia and tried to kill us both."

"Your friend did that?"

THE HOUSEWIFE

Olivia glanced at Brock, wondering where he was going with his tale. It was strange to hear him refer to Yara as a friend after so long too. He'd spent months denying his connection to her, making it seem like their bond was severed. Now, he was acting like it had been there all along. It made her a little uneasy. But Brock looked calm as he nodded.

"She did. She was very unwell. She had a severe problem with drinking and drugs... she was in withdrawal. And when she was faced with saving herself or saving others... She chose herself. I never saw her as a bad person before, but I changed my mind. I never pictured our paths going so far from one another. We didn't spend much time together, especially not in recent years. We grew up, went down our own paths... but I never pictured hers being so dark. I guess what I'm saying is that people are complicated, and people can change, sometimes for the worse. You can still care for your brother and acknowledge that he's got bad in him. You can still love him and know that it's for the best that he is put in prison. The friend I mentioned... She's on the run right now, and I'm hoping that someone catches her and puts her behind bars. It's not just what I want... It's a necessity. It doesn't mean I don't care. It just means that it's the right thing for everybody."

Olivia felt her throat tighten. She hadn't heard Brock be so honest about his feelings on Yara before. Not even after their call with Jonathan. But she could see him letting it all go, saying it as it was to get Matt on their side. She couldn't help admiring his bravery, and she felt proud that he had pushed through his own issues to help their case. She was sure it was going to be necessary to get Matt to complete the task.

"Thank you," Matt said after a moment, his eyes full of sorrow. "I won't let you down. I'll get him talking."

"You're doing the right thing," Olivia said with a reassuring smile. "And it'll be over soon, we hope. Just one phone call. That's all we need for now. Take it one step at a time, and we can finish this horrible mess."

Matt nodded, taking a deep breath. "And then maybe I'll finally feel free. I can do this."

Olivia and Brock waited, holding their breath. Time wasn't on their side, but patience was the only way they were going to get through the phone call. Matt needed to do it in his own time or he'd likely choke.

After a long minute, he sucked in air and then hit the call button. He put the speaker on and the ringing of the call filled the otherwise silent room. It rang once. Twice. Three times. Matt glanced at Olivia for reassurance and she gave him a thumbs up, trying to stop him from panicking. She needed him to stay focused on the task. But the phone continued to ring without anyone answering. When the call finally died out, Matt's body visibly deflated in relief.

"I guess he's not free," Matt said.

"Call again," Brock said firmly. Matt squirmed.

"He probably doesn't want to talk to me…"

"You need to keep trying. I'm sure he'll pick up eventually," Brock pushed. Matt wavered, but then he did as he was told. He started the call again, Olivia and Brock returning to silence to give way for Matt to take center stage. Olivia held her breath. One ring. Two. Three. Four… Olivia thought he might not pick up again. But then there was a crackle of static on the other end of the line and Olivia heard a long, irritable sigh from Matt's brother.

"Well, look who came crawling back to me. Long time no see, bro," Danny drawled. The sound of his voice made Olivia turn cold inside. He certainly didn't sound like a good man. Matt swallowed, anxiety written all over his face.

"I know, man. I'm sorry that I left things for so long… I was angry with you for so long, and I didn't know what else to do."

"So you walked away from me. Like a coward."

"I… I regretted it after," Matt said, clearly trying to keep the conversation on track. "I thought about calling you so many times. It's taken me this long to work up the courage… I guess I thought you wouldn't want to talk to me."

"Well, you were right."

"Danny… Come on, man…"

THE **HOUSEWIFE**

"Look, I don't have the patience right now to deal with whatever emotional revelation you're having. I'm not in the mood to kiss and make up."

"I just want a few minutes of your time…"

"Not now, Matt. I don't have time to talk to you. Just leave me alone. It's what you do best."

"No, wait!" Matt cried, panic crossing his face. "Tell me what's going on with you. You seem… stressed."

There was a long pause on the other end of the line. Then Danny cleared his throat.

"I'm fine."

"I don't think so," Matt said, a little breathless, but finally getting into the swing of the conversation. Olivia could see him digging his fingernails into his palm, trying to calm himself. "Maybe I can help you. I'm your big brother."

"You kind of forfeited that role when you cut me off."

"Come on, Danny. You know you put me in a bad position. You put my life completely off track. I'm really struggling over here. The least you can do is acknowledge what you did."

Danny scoffed. "I thought this was an apology, Matt. Well, it's not a very good one. Didn't Mom teach you any manners? Stop being such a baby and telling yourself that your bad luck has anything to do with me. It's not my problem that you can't get a job. Or a girlfriend for that matter. You never could! Stop blaming me for the fact that you're a loser and leave me alone."

Matt's face hardened. Olivia mouthed at him, telling him to stay calm, but it was too late. Matt clearly had something to say for himself.

"You never change, do you? Still an asshole, clearly."

Danny barked out a short laugh.

"Then why are you calling, huh? Were you expecting me to have changed? Well, you certainly haven't. You're still a butt-hurt loser with no life, and you're trying to make out like that's my fault. Now leave me alone. I told you, I'm busy."

Matt looked ready to end the call right there, but one long look from Brock stopped him from doing it. He took a steadying breath, composing himself.

"Danny…"

"What now? Going to insult me again or kiss my butt like a suck-up? Pick a lane."

Matt breathed in hard.

"I'm not running off again. You're a pain in the ass, but you're still my brother. You're my family. I always looked out for you before and I can again. God knows no one else is going to do it. You might act tough, but without me, I know you're on your own. No one else cares about you after what you put them through, so don't act like I'm the problem. I'm the only one still trying to have your back."

"I don't need this…"

"Don't push me away. You owe me that much. Tell me what's going on with you. Let me back in. Please."

There was a stretch of silence on the other end of the line. Olivia and Brock exchanged a glance. Danny was acting shifty for sure. But was it related to the case, or was he simply a bad guy in a bad place? Was he always so cold, or were they catching him at rock bottom? It was hard to tell, but Olivia hoped they were about to find out. Danny sighed deeply.

"There are some things you can't help with, brother. I'm not dragging you into my mess. Not this time."

"I want you to," Matt said. He sounded earnest as he spoke, slowly sitting down on the armchair to talk to him. "I want to help."

"Nah. Not this time. You know… you're not wrong. You're the only one who ever really cared about me." He paused. "I know I'm not easy to love, so you did me a solid there. But I'm letting you go from all that now. For your own sake."

"I don't understand…"

"Just look out for yourself for once, yeah? Forget what I said before, you'll find someone. The girls around here don't deserve you anyway. You can do better, man. Maybe you should finally skip town and try something else. I don't know what keeps you here."

"You know the answer to that. *You* keep me here."

Danny laughed cruelly on the other end of the line. "Oh, Matt. That's so pathetic. It's a good thing that's about to change. There won't be anything keeping you here after tonight."

THE **HOUSEWIFE**

"What are you talking about?"

"I'm leaving town too. And I'll be ditching this number, so don't even try to come looking for me. I'm done with this place and everyone in it."

"Why? Why would you do that?"

Danny chuckled. "Oh, you'll find out why soon enough. I'm not hiding who I am anymore. I don't think I can. But if you think I ruined your reputation before, you'll definitely want to keep your distance this time."

"You're not making any sense..."

"I'm making perfect sense. You just don't have the context yet. But you will soon. Goodbye for now, brother. If you want to hear about me again, I guess you'll have to read the papers."

"Danny—"

The line went dead. Matt's eyes were frantic as he looked between Olivia and Brock for answers.

"What was he talking about? I don't understand any of what he just said..."

"I think he's telling you he's done something bad," Olivia said. "Or he's about to."

"And then he's going to make a run for it," Brock said. "Matt, we're going to need your brother's address."

Matt's eyes were wild and frantic.

"I should come with you... he sounded strange. What if he hurts himself?"

"Being near your brother now is too dangerous, Matt. I'm more concerned about him hurting someone else. We need that address," Olivia said firmly. Matt wiped sweat from his brow, swallowing.

"Okay... I'll give you the address. But please... make sure he's okay. I'm worried about him. Arrest him if you have to... but please, don't kill him."

Olivia wasn't worried for Danny's safety in the slightest. The entire call had made her uneasy. And the more she thought about it, the more it sounded like he'd done something he shouldn't have. What did that mean for the people around him? If he was their killer, then he was a very dangerous man.

And when dangerous men were on edge, people died.

CHAPTER TWENTY-THREE

THE RACE WAS ON. BROCK DROVE THEM AS FAST AS HE could to the home of Danny Henderson. Olivia knew there was no way they could be sure they had the right man, but his instability was so obvious to her that she felt in her gut that he was the one. Everything about him fit the profile of the killers—his background in security, his lewd past, his troublemaking for everyone around him. They still didn't know who the assistant was, or how much of the killing was down to him, but it felt like the answers would be waiting for them at the house.

The house he was planning to flee.

"If he's the killer, he'll be armed. Should we call for backup?" Olivia asked. Brock shook his head.

"We can handle this. We don't have time for backup—he sounds like he's about to skip town. God knows what he's done now, but I feel like this must be something different. He sounded like he was implying that he'd done something he can't come back from. Which means what, exactly? That he's slipped up? Maybe someone saw something he did, or found out a secret he was keeping? Something that maybe unveils him as the killer…"

"Which likely means he killed someone close to him," Olivia breathed. She suddenly felt sure that whatever waited for them at Danny's house was going to be troubling. She also felt sure that they were going to be too late to stop another death from occurring.

The house wasn't far from Matt's, but the drive felt far too long for Olivia's liking. Her heart was hammering hard in her chest, making her feel a little nauseous. But she had no time to focus on it. The second they parked outside the modest house with the neat lawn, Olivia felt her unease grow. There was no car in front of the house, and Olivia suspected that Danny had already left. Brock led the way to the front door and hammered his fists on the door.

"FBI, open up!"

There was no response from inside, but Olivia wasn't surprised. She had a horrible feeling that if there was anyone left inside the house, they weren't breathing any longer. There was a stillness in the air, like nothing could possibly survive the house they were desperately trying to get inside.

Brock knocked loudly again, but with no answer. Olivia moved to the window to look inside and her stomach twisted.

"Brock, I can see a body on the floor."

Brock didn't need any more encouragement to butt his way inside the house. He threw his shoulder up against the door until it gave, the lock busting inward and allowing them inside. With her gun in her hand, Olivia rushed inside to back Brock up. But the house was silent, and Olivia was sure that Danny was long gone.

The body belonged to another woman. She was sprawled out on the living room floor, fresh blood still staining the carpet as it drained from her body. She was riddled with knife wounds, and

THE **HOUSEWIFE**

she wasn't long dead. Olivia suspected, given the location of the kill, that they were looking at Danny Henderson's wife.

"He's the one," Olivia murmured. "It has to be him."

"Is this his partner for the killings?" Brock mused, still on high alert, looking around for signs of someone still in the house. "And if so, why has he killed her?"

"Perhaps she threatened to end it all. She was going to expose him, maybe. But he must have known this would be the end of his reign of terror. Killing someone linked to him... that identifies him as the killer, especially given his background. He's smart enough to know we'll be on to him now. That's why he left in such a hurry. Took the car and is no doubt getting the hell away while he still can..."

Olivia trailed off as she noticed something in the corner of the room. Something that didn't look like it belonged there.

"Brock..." Olivia whispered. "There's a camera in here."

Brock looked up at where Olivia was staring. The camera wasn't concealed in any way. It was as though it had always been there, but Olivia thought that seemed odd. Why would anyone have cameras in their own home, watching them? Maybe it was a paranoia thing. Or perhaps it was something else that fed Danny's sexual perversions. Perhaps he himself liked to be observed, to be center stage at all times. It wouldn't surprise her, considering the narcissistic tendencies he'd displayed. There was no doubt in her mind now that Danny was the one they had been chasing since Valentine's Day.

"Brock... if this camera is on, then there will be evidence of Danny killing his wife," Olivia murmured. Then she jumped as she heard a laugh booming out of a speaker beside the TV. Olivia turned to look at it, frowning. What on Earth was going on in this house?

"I'm sure by the time you get the evidence you need, I'll be long gone," Danny's voice said from the speaker, followed by another chuckle. "I had a feeling someone would be closing in on me soon, but I've got to say, you got here faster than I expected. I wonder if my brother has anything to do with that. It *does* seem a little suspicious to me that he called just as I was wrapping up at home with my dear old wife... and in the middle of a murder investigation where the subject is me... I don't know why he thought he could stab me in the back like that and get away with it. He knows I'm the smart one in the family."

"Danny... where are you?" Olivia asked. He chuckled again.

"It must be so frustrating for you... being played by someone smarter than you. It's funny how you're looking for me so desperately, but I can see you *right now*. Yes, I've got a good look at you, Olivia Knight. And yes, I know who you are. You thought I wouldn't be keeping tabs on the FBI investigation in my town? You threatened my entire setup... but I got what I wanted here. Those women fed a hunger I've had for *such* a long time. And now that my dearest wife is dead, there's nothing keeping me here. It's time to move on. Onwards and upwards, as they say. I wonder what I'll achieve next..."

"Why did you kill your wife? Why would you keep doing this?" Brock asked.

"She also threatened my setup, Brock. She found out what I was up to... and about time, too. I've been killing under her nose for years. All those business trips she thought I was taking, I was just doing my 'work' elsewhere. I'm obviously not talking about security installation here. But as soon as I started killing closer to home, I knew there would be risks. She threatened to hand me over to the police, but I disagreed. Because I'm not done yet. I have so much more that I want to achieve. This is only the beginning. For example, I've never tried to kill an FBI agent before..."

"It's not too late to turn yourself in," Olivia said coldly. Danny laughed.

"Why would I do that when I've already gotten away with it? You won't catch up to me now. Unless I decide to pop back and pay my brother a visit... I prefer killing women, but killing a traitor like him would be almost as sweet. Or maybe I'm already at his house. Maybe I'm way ahead of you yet again. Wouldn't that be a twist?"

Olivia felt a dreadful pool in her stomach. They needed to warn Matt. She knew that Danny could just be playing games with them, but it was a risk they couldn't afford to take. They needed backup and they needed a plan on how they were going to catch Danny. It would be easier trying to catch smoke as it wisped away from them.

"I think I'm done here. It was fun to watch you squirm a little, but I'm bored of this now. Onwards and upwards, right? Don't bother coming to look for me. You're just wasting your own time as well as mine," Danny said. "Goodbye for now. And good luck clearing up my mess."

Danny's voice left the room, and Olivia was about to speak to Brock when alarms started blaring loudly through the house. Olivia clamped her hands over her ears, gritting her teeth. No doubt it was a final gesture from Danny to show off what he was capable of. After all, manipulating security was his specialty, and setting off some alarms wasn't beyond his capabilities. But cheap tricks like that wouldn't stop Olivia from catching him. Now that they knew who they were looking for, she would be hot on his tail. She was determined that he wouldn't ever get an opportunity to kill again. They would call in back up to make sure Matt was safe and to deal with Danny's wife.

And meanwhile, Olivia would hunt him down, no matter what it took.

CHAPTER TWENTY-FOUR

CHAOS FOLLOWED DANNY HENDERSON'S DISAPPEARANCE. Olivia and Brock called the local police to process the crime scene and to ensure that Matt was protected. Danny's threats turned out to be hollow when Matt made it to the police station unharmed, but it was clear that he was scared and out of sorts. Being escorted away by the police must have been an awful shock for him, though Olivia was glad that he hadn't been told about the threat on his life from his own brother.

Now, Olivia and Brock were keen to speak to him again. Someone brought Matt a cup of coffee while Olivia and Brock sat down with him at the police station. He held it with shaking hands, barely able to sip from the cup without spilling it.

THE HOUSEWIFE

"We're going to need your help even more now," Brock explained to him. "We know now that Danny is the killer. He's responsible for the deaths of at least five women in total, along with a possible assistant that we haven't yet identified."

"I just can't believe it," Matt said. His teeth were chattering even though the room wasn't cold. "I never thought he would do something so awful… not to his wife, for sure… Hayley was a good woman. He loved her at one time, I know he did. He might not seem capable of it, but he used to look at her like she was everything to him… back when he still had a shred of decency."

"Do you think she knew what Danny was doing all along?"

Matt shook his head, shock still resting on his face. "I can't see how she would let him get away with it if she knew. She was very strong-willed, and wouldn't let anyone walk all over her. She was a pacifist, and had very strong morals. I think that must have been why he killed her in the end… she threatened his plans."

"That's exactly what he said to us," Olivia said, feeling a cold shiver running down her spine. She fought it off by shrugging her shoulders uncomfortably. "What we need from you now is anything that could be useful… Do you think there's somewhere he would go to feel safe? Like a base he could hide in if things went wrong for him, a place he would go to as a last resort?"

Matt chewed his lip. "I don't know… he's not a sentimental person. I don't think there are many places that would hold meaning to him… he hasn't been home in years so my parents are out of the question. He's smart enough not to visit them anyway. Unless… unless he wanted to kill them too. Before, I don't think he would've risked it. But everything has changed now… you don't think he'd attack our parents next, do you?"

Olivia glanced at Brock. It was entirely possible that Danny would be more unhinged than ever now. With his identity revealed to them, there wasn't much stopping him from going after people that he was clearly connected to. If he felt like his time was running out, maybe he would lose control entirely. And according to Matt, Danny hadn't had much of a relationship with their family. If he wanted anyone dead, it could be them. Brock swallowed.

"I'll make some calls. Make sure your family is made aware and are taken to safety," Brock assured Matt. Matt nodded in response, his skin paling. He clutched his coffee anxiously.

"Don't worry about them right now. They're safe," Olivia said gently. "All you need to do is think. Think where he might go."

Matt wavered. "I really don't know… we haven't spoken in nearly two years, have we? All I can think about is my Dad's old fishing cabin… it's remote, it's off the beaten track and not many people would know where to find it… but that doesn't feel right to me. Like I said, he's not sentimental. I just don't think he would go somewhere connected to my parents."

"Well, I suppose we can look into it if there's nothing else… but dig deep, Matt. Your brother is a smart man. He's cunning and cold. Think outside the box… you're nothing like him, but if anyone can get inside his head, it's you. You knew him better than anyone else, he said it himself."

Matt stared into space, his expression pained and tired. He worried at his lip until Olivia saw a bead of blood blossoming from it. He sighed deeply.

"I think you're right. He's cunning and cold. I don't think there's a place he would turn to. But I do think he would have a plan in place. He knows how to play the system. He's been doing it for years, always getting away with things he shouldn't. He knows how to get away without leaving a paper trail, and he certainly knows better than to use his bank accounts or any ID. If I was in his shoes… if I had been killing for a long time and getting away with it… I might be cocky, but I would also have a backup plan."

"A new identity?" Olivia prompted. Matt nodded.

"I think he would be prepared to cut and run. You said he took the car, but he will have dumped it by now, no doubt. Maybe he had a car stored away somewhere for a getaway. He wouldn't be against changing his appearance, even surgically."

"Unsentimental," Olivia said. Matt nodded.

"Exactly. If it means not having to go to prison… there's not much he wouldn't do. I've seen him do things in the past that scared me to death. Once when we were kids, he threw himself in front of a car to get out of school. I wouldn't put it past him to maim himself to change his appearance, either. In the long run, I think that'll be in the cards. But for now, he won't be going anywhere without some kind of fake ID. He's changed his name once, he could do it again. He will maybe have back up bank accounts ready to go. But failing that... if he needs to lie low somewhere, I think he'll hide in plain sight. If he's waiting for things to die down and he's without a phone, without cash, without everything he might need... I don't know. He doesn't exactly have friends to rely on or a place to stay. He won't have anyone he can trust not to turn him in certainly. It's hard to picture where he might go."

Olivia weighed it up in her mind. If she was going somewhere to be anonymous, where would she pick? Somewhere where people didn't ask too many questions about identity, who offered help without judgment. Olivia's mind was ticking over.

"Was your brother ever religious, Matt?"

He shook his head fervently. "Definitely not. In fact, he often mocked people for their beliefs. I guess he believed his fate was in his own hands, not God's."

Olivia hummed to herself. She had pictured a church as a place of sanctuary to a man like Danny in his moment of desperation, but if he was truly a non-believer, she didn't think it would be his first port of call. She closed her eyes and thought harder. Where else could a person turn to when there was nowhere else?

Her eyes snapped open.

"Do you think he might try a homeless shelter?"

Matt's eyes widened. "Maybe... I think he would do almost anything to blend in, to make sure no one was looking for him there... but it's like you said. He's smart, he's unpredictable... he could have almost anything up his sleeve."

"That's true. But we have to start somewhere. And though he tried to tell us otherwise, he's backed into a corner. He's not going anywhere far anytime soon. There are police patrolling, looking for the car he left his house in. By morning everyone will know what he's done. The smart thing for him to do would be to lie low. And that's how we'll nail him when he doesn't expect it."

Matt's eyes were sad as he nodded. Olivia didn't want to sound too enthusiastic in front of him, given that they were talking about catching his brother, but if she was a step closer to Danny Henderson, then she couldn't hide that she was pleased. He didn't deserve to get away with it. He was a monster, a creature that fed on misery from the shadows.

But Olivia wasn't afraid of the dark.

Brock returned from making his call and Olivia got to her feet. Matt looked panicked.

"Where are you going?"

"To the homeless shelter," Olivia said. "To see if we can find your brother."

CHAPTER TWENTY-FIVE

O**LIVIA HAD NEVER SEEN** D**ANNY** H**ENDERSON IN THE** flesh, but his face was burned into her mind as they made their way to the homeless shelter. He hadn't had much time to get away from them, and yet Olivia knew every second he was let loose to live, no one was safe. He had proved just how dangerous he was, and now it was time to put a stop to him. The homeless shelter was a shot in the dark, but Olivia had a feeling he hadn't left town yet. That's what he would believe they would think. Olivia knew that the way to catch someone like Danny was to turn everything they thought they knew on its head. That's how they'd catch him unawares.

Olivia was glad that Danny was cocky enough to believe he might have outsmarted them. That would give them the advantage when they found him. *If* they found him. Olivia silently prayed that she had made the right decision to follow her instinct to the homeless shelter. The more time they wasted, the more time Danny would have to plot how to escape them for good.

Brock drove cautiously, but fast, trying to get them there sooner. He hadn't said much since Olivia had pitched her idea, and she could tell he had doubts.

"Do you really think he'll be here?" Brock asked eventually. "I get that it's a place to blend in… but it just seems so reckless. Trying to blend in here, in the town where he lives."

"I know. It's so reckless that he will see it as smart," Olivia said. "We have to remember that he's running on adrenaline right now. His ideas are going to be wilder, more out of the box. He thinks he's sent us on a wild goose chase, that we'll never look for him somewhere close to home. But he's trying too hard to be smart. I think there's a good chance he's here. And if he isn't… well, it's back to the drawing board."

Brock reached over to squeeze Olivia's knee. "I'm not doubting you, I promise. You don't often get these kinds of things wrong. I just hope that you're right. We need this man behind bars."

Olivia nodded. "Hey I wanted to say… those things you told Matt back at his house… I'm proud of you. I know how hard this whole Yara thing has been for you. But now that you're not thinking so black and white about it all, I think I understand you a bit better."

Brock sighed. "Well, I guess there's no getting away from the fact that I still care about what happens to her. That's the curse of caring about someone, right? Always being prepared to be hurt by them?"

"I guess so, on some level. But I don't want you thinking that it's like that for everyone."

"It is, though. Everyone is capable of screwing you over. I guess I just didn't think she'd ever make that choice. And I know deep down that she's not all bad, but she's not good either. Oh, I don't know. She runs circles in my head. I just want to know she's safe… and that she hasn't hurt anyone else."

THE HOUSEWIFE

"Hopefully she is. I can't see the Gamemaster hurting her. Not if she's part of her grand schemes somehow."

"I think we're all a part of that mad woman's grand schemes in some way. I dread to think what that means for us," Brock muttered. He turned the steering wheel and they swerved into an almost deserted parking lot. "This is the place. How do we want to do this?"

Olivia chewed her lip. "We don't want to go in all guns blazing and scare everyone. There's a lot of vulnerable people in this building, few of whom like cops, and I don't think Danny will be against using them as protection for himself. We need to go in quietly and see if we can spot him before he even knows we're present. If he's here, I don't think he'll be too hard to spot. I don't know about you, but I think his face is going to haunt me for a while."

Olivia and Brock got out of the car and crept through the parking lot in the dark. There wasn't a soul in sight. Through the window of the community center, Olivia could see people lining up to collect dinner. She didn't spot Danny's face among them right away, but when she did, she locked in on him. He had dyed his hair dark to cover up the blonde, and he had facial hair unlike in his photos, but Olivia could still see the family resemblance with Matt easily. He had the same smug smile she had seen in the photo of him and Matt, a cruelness in his eyes. She felt a moment of satisfaction. A man so smart, so calculated, easily tracked down by them. He wouldn't be smug for much longer. Olivia turned back to Brock.

"I think we're going to have a chase on our hands."

"Then how do we play it? Are we still both going inside? Or should we try and keep the doors covered?"

"I can see an emergency exit on the other side of the hall. I think if he makes a break for it, he'll go through there. One of us should cover it and the other should try to flush him out."

"Sounds like a plan. I'll go around. You've got this handled," Brock said. He pressed his hand to her cheek gently. "Good luck. Not that you need it."

"We've got this," Olivia told him. Saying it aloud was like an affirmation to herself. And she didn't feel anxious parting ways with Brock this time. Every time they were separated during a mission, she felt her heart squeeze. They'd had so many close calls before, becoming far too familiar with near death. But Olivia believed this time that everything would be okay. They had their guy. She'd like to see how he'd outsmart them out of this one.

Olivia rushed to the front of the building to enter and begin the chase. She acted casual as she pushed inside. She was almost stopped by a member of staff, but she quietly flashed her badge and was allowed to continue on through to the main hall. She went unnoticed as she entered, everyone's attention on the dinner line.

Aside from Danny's.

He looked up as Olivia entered the room. She watched a quick flicker of panic cross his face and he leapt to his feet, already making a break for the emergency exit. Olivia broke into a sprint, closing the distance between them faster than Danny could anticipate. She watched as panic took over him, his head darting over his shoulder as he slammed through the exit and shut it behind him. It only slowed Olivia down for a moment, but she hoped those precious seconds wouldn't allow him to slip away.

She barreled through the exit. She could see Brock chasing Danny down. Panic seemed to have made him faster, and he headed for the parking lot. Olivia continued the pursuit, her feet pounding hard into the ground. She reached for her gun. She wouldn't take any chances. Danny was a dangerous man, armed or not. They couldn't afford to let him slip by.

Brock and Danny rounded a corner and Olivia lost sight of them for a moment. When they came back into view, she saw Danny throw a wild punch at Brock. He cried out as the punch landed on his nose. Olivia gritted her teeth and rushed toward them. Danny was wild and desperate, trying to punch Brock again, but Olivia wouldn't let him lay another hand on him.

She threw her weight into Danny and both of them tumbled to the ground. Olivia heard the breath leaving Danny's chest, a whooshing sound escaping him. But he didn't stop trying to escape. He writhed beneath her, clawing at her like an animal. But Olivia wasn't about to let him go.

"You're done," she snapped, pinning one of his arms down with her knee. "You're under arrest for five counts of first-degree murder. Anything you say can and will be used against you in a court of law. You have a right to an attorney. If you cannot afford an attorney, one will be appointed for you."

"How the hell did you find me?" Danny snarled. "I got away! I got away with it!"

"Clearly, you didn't," Brock said as he recovered from the punch to his nose. "You bit off a little more than you could chew, didn't you? But where's your associate? We know you have one. If you cooperate, we can make life a little easier for you."

"I won't talk," Danny snapped as Olivia handcuffed him. Brock shrugged.

"Shame. I guess we'll just have to make sure you never leave prison again."

Danny's lips curled into a snarl. "We both know that I was never getting out anyway. No deal you're willing to cut me is worth enough."

"See how you feel a year down the line. I hear prison gets old fast," Olivia said. She hauled Danny to his feet. "Now, what say we find you a holding cell?"

CHAPTER TWENTY-SIX

"This should be an interesting conversation," Brock murmured as he and Olivia watched Danny Henderson through the two-way glass. It had been twelve hours since they'd taken him into custody, giving Olivia and Brock a chance to rest. It had been a whirlwind week, and Olivia had slept well knowing that Danny was behind bars.

But he had transformed in their twelve hours apart. He didn't look like the angry, frightened man they'd hunted down at the homeless shelter. This man was closer to what Olivia had expected from him—cold and smug and dangerous. There was a glint in his eye as he stared ahead, knowing they were watching him from behind the glass. When he lifted one handcuffed hand to wave at them, Olivia felt a shiver roll down her spine.

THE **HOUSEWIFE**

"You think he'll talk?" Olivia asked. She knew they had enough evidence to pin everything on him now—everything was adding up to point in his direction. But there were still things they didn't know, or things they weren't certain of. She was counting on Danny feeling talkative to fill in some of the gaps.

"I think he'll talk," Brock said. "I don't think a guy like him can help himself. He's desperate to show off. It must've been killing him to keep it under wraps this whole time. That's probably the reason he didn't work alone. He needed to be perceived, to have someone acknowledge his brilliance."

"If only we knew who his admirer was," Olivia said with a sigh. "I doubt we'll get that out of him."

"You never know. It's worth a shot."

"I guess we'd better try," Olivia said. She let Brock lead the way into the interrogation room, pushing aside her doubts for the moment. As she sat down opposite Danny, he awkwardly slowly clapped her entrance with his handcuffed hands.

"Well, I've got to say you two impressed me. I've been dodging cops for years, but you two? You surprised me," Danny said.

"I wish we could say the same about you," Brock said, quirking an eyebrow. "Five people died in five weeks because of you. Don't you think your skills could go to better use?"

"I think they went to perfect use," Danny said with a smile. "The thing about being smarter than everyone else is that it gets boring. I remember being in school, listening to all those kiss-ass teachers gushing about how well I was doing, how I was really going places, how I could do anything I wanted with my life. And I guess that gave me a little bit of an ego. I got tired of running around trying to follow other people's rules, trying to fit in. I knew I was above that. I decided to look deep inside myself and ask... what is it that I really want? And somewhere along the way, I realized I wanted a challenge. And what's more challenging than pulling off the perfect murder?"

"We have you for five counts of murder, possibly six. Did you kill the young starlet in Atlantic City?" Olivia asked. Danny's smile only grew wider.

"I did. And I didn't even plan that one. I just had a good opportunity with the power cut. I could've orchestrated that myself, if I had wanted to... but I wasn't there to kill that weekend. I was there to gamble, to relax a little. But how could I resist when the situation was so perfect? She never saw it coming."

"So that's six. You don't seem particularly interested in hiding what you've done," Brock said, his expression hard. Danny shrugged.

"What's the point now? You've already got me for five. It's like you said... I'm never seeing outside of a prison again. I might as well let the world know what I've done."

"I see," Brock said, disgust written all over his face. "Then why don't you tell us about the rest?"

Danny leaned back in his seat, looking far too relaxed for the conversation they were having. "Let me see... I'll have to think about this, I sort of lost count. I started out just killing whenever I went on a vacation... I'd find excuses to go away just so I could make a kill. It started just with stabbings in parks, in alleyways, or out in the open in the night. From there, I learned and I adapted. I would stake out a place and kill whoever was there."

"So they weren't all women?"

Danny smirked. "Most were. There's something so much sweeter about killing a woman. The way they scream, the fear in their eyes... they think they're finally in a place they can relax, inside their home. But I like to remind them that there's nowhere on Earth where they'd be safe from me."

Olivia clenched her fist under the table, keeping her face level. Anger surged through her, but she knew that Danny was simply looking for a reaction. That was something that she wasn't willing to give to him.

"How many have you killed?"

Danny shrugged. "Oh, I lose count. Dozens, maybe? But it's like I said before... Being clever can be boring. At first, I wasn't planning in advance. But my job in security made me curious about what I was capable of. Could I disable an entire system without being caught? Could I enter someone's home without being spotted and end their life? I was curious about how far I could take it. So I started slacking off at work, using my time to case houses that I'd done installations for. I hacked the camera systems, easy-peasy. And I'm sure you know by now that I had my fun with that too."

"You mean when you uploaded pornographic videos of a couple to the internet and got you and your brother fired?" Brock asked. Danny clicked his fingers.

"Bingo. You did do your homework. Matt never forgave me for that. Which is why I knew something was up when he called me out of the blue. It pays to be suspicious in my line of work. Anyway, I digress. The security systems were my own personal spin on the killings. No one was giving me any prizes for my style before that—and I wanted to be remembered, to be feared. I started to build my legacy, but I was still avoiding killing too close to home, especially after I got married. My dear wife would never have approved of my… activities. But I had her fooled pretty well. And everyone else. Even when I got caught out the first time, I got off lucky. The sun tends to shine on me for the most part. I've gotten good at getting on people's good side. Comes in handy when you're causing trouble left right and center."

"What made you start killing closer to home, then?" Olivia asked. Danny shrugged.

"It got boring again. I decided that I needed to do something bigger to catch the thrill I've been chasing this whole time. It had been a good while since my last kill, and I wanted to do something that would make it more… satisfying. I decided that the kills would be pretty much back-to-back, that I would only target women, that they'd all be nearby. And most of all, I wanted to watch them first. I spent *hours*. I followed Kristen around the most. She made it so easy."

He said it with a lascivious grin that made Olivia bristle with rage. But she made no move to betray her emotions. He didn't deserve that from her.

"She was so cute, always heading to the park with her son or to her yoga class or her favorite coffee shop. It was all so mundane… but she wasn't. I loved watching her. Especially after I hacked into her computer. I got to see her in ways that not many people did…

at home, off duty, when she thought no one was watching. But I was. It almost seemed a shame to kill her after everything we'd been through together… but the thrill had never been so big. The stakes had never been higher…"

"What about the Young family? How did you pull it off?" Olivia asked.

Danny snorted. "You make it sound like it was hard. They barely put up a fight. I mean, Nell did complicate things. I had my sights set on Karen, not her. But when she came home earlier than planned, it turned out to be an added thrill to the whole thing. Nell wailed like a baby when she saw Karen go down… so I put her out of her misery before she knew what had hit her. And in a big house like that, no one outside was going to hear a thing. They make such easy targets, rich people. I guess I should have tried something more challenging. But I took a risk by operating closer to home. I guess it didn't pay off. But it was worth it… I had the time of my life."

Olivia often felt strong hate toward the killers they caught, but her hate for Danny was on another level. The smugness of him was almost more than she could bear. It never failed to surprise her how dark some people could become, how low they'd sink with no remorse. Her only solace was knowing he'd rot in prison for the rest of his life.

"What about the stolen goods? What did you do with those? I'm guessing they were more of a trophy for your side piece? Your partner in crime?"

Danny smirked at Olivia. "I'm not telling you anything about my associate. You thought you had all the answers when you caught me, didn't you? Well, you don't know half of what we pulled off. And you never will. By now, my associate will be out of the country."

"You can't mind game us, Danny. We're the ones with the power here," Brock said. Danny chuckled.

"Then why all of the questions? I have something you need. You have nothing to offer me for my information. So you caught me… I'll happily tell you my side of the story. Someone should know exactly what I managed to pull off. But I have no incentive

THE HOUSEWIFE

to tell you more. I guess you're just going to have to figure that out alone… or not at all."

"I can take a stab at it," Olivia said. "You keep telling us about the boredom… how you needed something to add some flavor to the tasks at hand. And what better way than to include someone in your work? It needed to be someone who wouldn't judge you for what you wanted to do… but I guess someone knowing your secret was always going to be a risk, and that excited you more, didn't it?"

Danny shrugged. "Maybe."

"I think you and this woman hit it off. She started coming with you to make your kills. But she had ambitions of her own. She craved a rich lifestyle, which is why you targeted such rich women. She was also a kleptomaniac. She stole for the fun of it, but she was selective about what she took. She wanted to own beautiful things, things she'd never had before. The value meant something to her, but so did the beauty of the items. And together, you felt like a power couple. She never got her hands dirty herself, but hey, if it made you happy, it made her happy. You never told her about your perversions, though. That would be a step too far for her. Killing was fine, but your obsession with other women? Maybe that would've sent her over the edge. Especially given that she's deeply in love with you…"

Olivia could see that her analysis was angering him, but she didn't care. In fact, she wanted to rile him up. What could he do about it now, anyway? He couldn't hurt her or anyone else when he was handcuffed to a table. She smiled at him.

"This side chick of yours… Did she ever get angry with you? It must've been *so* frustrating, you being in a marriage to someone else. I bet jealousy was getting the better of her. And as your killings got more intense, so did her feelings. I think she gave you an ultimatum, didn't she? Did she threaten to tell your wife about the affair? About everything? And the question is, did she follow through on her threats? Is that why you were forced to kill her, hmm? Or are you just that cold?"

Danny snorted. "You think you've got me figured out."

"Maybe not yet, but I've got time. Something you don't have the luxury of. I don't think your lover left the country at all. I don't think she would abandon you. And no one knows you've been caught yet… So what will she do when she finds out? She'll be so pleased that you followed through with your promise of getting rid of your wife. Maybe she will even try to help you out here. Because here's the thing… I know guys like you. You like to be the smartest man in any room you walk into. It gives you power. So I'll bet this side chick of yours is dumb as hell. You were the brains behind the whole thing, as you keep reminding us. I reckon she's sticking around. I wouldn't be surprised if we come across her soon. And then at least the two of you can go down together."

Danny's jaw was set in anger. Olivia cocked her head to the side, challenging him to fight her further.

"Am I close to the truth, Danny? You're not very good at hiding your emotions, has anyone ever told you that? Or is it just because you've been outsmarted for the first time?"

"Just leave her be. She didn't do anything," Danny snarled.

"Oh, but she did. She watched you murder at least four people. She was a witness and she chose to protect the killer. She might not do as much jail time as you, but she'll certainly be put in a cell for a good while. But don't worry. I'm sure she'll fit right in with all the killers and thieves. I hear that's the company she likes to keep."

Danny gritted his teeth, refusing to say anything further. Olivia turned to Brock.

"Do you think we should leave Danny to his thoughts? We've got a thief to catch."

"I think that's a better use of our time," Brock said with a smile. "I don't think we need to use any more brain power on this one."

The final blow seemed to devastate Danny the most. It was a sweet feeling, breaking down such a cruel man, insulting his intelligence when it was what he prided himself on most. As Olivia left the room, she felt liberated by their final interview. He might have been smart, but not quite smart enough. He would have to sit with that knowledge for the rest of his life.

And he'd have plenty of time to think about that in jail.

CHAPTER TWENTY-SEVEN

Danny Henderson didn't know it, but Olivia and Brock weren't following up on his associate. After a long discussion with the police and the FBI, it had been decided that the rest of the investigation could be handed over to the local authorities. Their killer had been caught, and though his associate was wanted as an accessory, Olivia and Brock had provided significant evidence to help the police finish the job. It was time for them to return home for some well-earned rest.

Belle Grove welcomed their return with open arms. Olivia felt ready to just melt into the sofa and fall asleep, but her stomach had been grumbling the whole drive home.

"I'm getting you a pizza," Brock insisted the moment they got through the door. "It'll only take twenty minutes to walk and grab one. Then we can get an early night."

"You're an angel," Olivia said, already making herself comfortable on the sofa. "Can I get a veggie supreme?"

He made a face. "Veggie? That sounds horrendous."

"That's fine, you won't be sharing it with me."

"Rude. But fine. It's your life you're ruining. I'll be getting a meat feast and actually enjoying my life."

"Good for you," Olivia yawned, too tired from the past week to put up much banter. Brock was soon out of the house on his way to get the pizzas. Olivia forced herself to stand up and go to the sink for a big glass of water. She hoped it might wake her up a bit.

But nothing woke her up more than the click of a gun behind her.

"Turn around. Slowly," a woman's voice told her. It was vaguely familiar to Olivia, though she couldn't place it. She turned slowly, assessing the situation. Their home had been broken into before they arrived home, and they hadn't noticed. Her assailant was a woman. They were looking for Danny's associate… it had to be her.

But when Olivia turned and saw who was pointing the gun at her, her breath caught in her throat.

"Sally?"

The woman slowly smiled. She looked a little different than when Olivia had last seen her at the reunion. Her brown bob was mussed and her clothes were rumpled, as if they'd been thrown on in a hurry. But it was unmistakably her. Olivia looked her up and down in horror.

"At least you remember my name this time," Sally said snidely. "I saw the way you fished around for it in your brain at the reunion… you'd forgotten all about me. You wouldn't be the first, but my God, it irritated me."

"Sally… What the hell is going on here?"

Sally scoffed. "All this interest in me all of a sudden… Now you're paying attention, right? I was never on your radar back in

THE **HOUSEWIFE**

school. We had half the same classes together, but you just acted like I didn't exist. I'm going to make sure you never forget me again. Not that you've got long left."

"I don't understand," Olivia said. It was an honest statement, and also one that would buy her some time. "What are you doing here? And how did you find me?"

"I'm here because I slipped through your fingers," Sally said, adjusting her grip on her pistol. "You caught Dan. Bad luck on his part. He's a genius, and he shouldn't be in a cell right now. But you just had to show off again, didn't you? The amazing Olivia Knight, always in the right place at the right time. Always trying to save the day. But not this time."

Olivia swallowed. "You're the associate. The thief."

Sally's smile grew wider. "Yes. I might not be the brains of the operation, but I certainly got what I wanted from the deal. A handsome boyfriend, for one, and a taste of luxury. Going jet-setting with Jules was one thing, but I had a hunger for something more. And when I met Dan, he knew just what I wanted. Stealing from those women while Danny sent them to their graves... I've never known a thrill like it."

"You're not a killer, Sally," Olivia said firmly, trying to keep her talking long enough for Brock to return.

Sally scoffed. "Of course, I never got my hands dirty myself... I wouldn't take that from Danny. But I suppose this is my act of revenge for what you did to him. And for all those years that I flew beneath your radar... you always thought you were too good for me."

"Sally... I assure you, I never thought that. I kept to myself at school. It wasn't anything personal. And that was over ten years ago now. What do you want me to say?"

"I don't want you to say anything," Sally said through gritted teeth. "In fact... you know what I want?" She pressed the gun beneath Olivia's chin and tilted it upwards. "I want some respect from you. And then I want to hear you scream as I end you for good. I want to walk a mile in Dan's shoes. He always told me how sweet killing feels..."

"You don't want to cross that line," Olivia whispered. Sally glared her down.

"You have no idea what I want. Do you know what an ordinary day looks like for me? *Closet renovations.* Not even the renovations themselves. I'm just an assistant for the company. Do you know how *boring* that is? You have no idea. Every day is an adventure for you, isn't it? Well, some of us have to look harder for our adventures. I started casing the houses for Danny. I'd accompany my boss to the homes—he was grooming me to be a saleswoman some day—and I'd tell him all about those snooty women and their expensive homes. I'd tell him the weak spots, and help him decide which women to target. *I* picked out Kayla *and* Kristen. They both treated me like I didn't *exist*, even as I walked around their homes. I wanted them gone, so Dan made it happen. If only we'd had more time… I was desperate to come for you next, Olivia. I guess I'm doing this one alone."

"Why? Because we weren't best pals at high school?" Olivia said incredulously. "You're a psycho."

Sally's nostrils flared. "You put my boyfriend away for *life!*"

"Because he murdered people, Sally."

"And good riddance to them! Everything was fine until you interfered. You ruined everything. We finally got his dumb wife out of the picture, and now I won't even get to enjoy the fact. Now move. I want to wait for your boyfriend to get home… so he can watch me blow your brains out in front of him."

Olivia knew she needed to take Sally down. There was no reasoning with her when she was so adamant to hate her. There was history there that Olivia couldn't even recall, a story Sally had made up to herself in her own head. How had this gotten so out of hand? Plenty of people had wanted Olivia dead before, but never someone she'd known once, never someone who had been harboring hate for years and years. Olivia could barely believe this had come back to bite her in the ass. But one thing was for sure. Sally—even armed with a gun—was no match for Olivia.

Sally shoved Olivia forward and as she was propelled forward, she ducked down, sweeping her legs out to catch Sally's ankles. Taken by surprise, Sally yelped and fell forward, but she didn't drop the gun. Olivia grabbed the gun and twisted it hard. Sally yelled in pain as her finger bent with the motion, her broken digit going lax on the trigger. Within a few moments, Olivia had twisted the gun from Sally's grip, leaving her yowling in agony.

"I didn't want to do that," Olivia said, turning the gun on Sally. "Put your hands in the air. You're under arrest."

Sally let out a feral scream and tried to dive at Olivia again, but Olivia wasn't having it. After all the woman had tried to put her through, she was no longer feeling merciful. She landed a punch low in Sally's stomach, doubling her over. Then she wrestled her to the ground until Sally was lying on her belly.

"Don't try anything else. It's not going to work and I don't want to break any other bones," Olivia said plainly. She pinned Sally's hands together as carefully as she could and grabbed the handcuffs that were still on her belt. She made a mental note to never be anywhere without them.

Sally was screaming in frustration and pain, trying to wriggle free, but it was finished. Olivia wasn't about to let her get away now. She was just catching her breath when the front door opened and Brock rushed into the room.

"What the hell is going on here?" Brock asked, almost dropping the pizza boxes. Olivia sighed, dusting herself off as she stood up straight.

"All you need to know is that Sally needs an escort to the police station."

"Sally from the reunion?" Brock said, blinking in confusion. Olivia grabbed Sally by the arm and hauled her to her feet, shrugging.

"Looks like it. Just another day on the job, right?"

CHAPTER TWENTY-EIGHT

"Well, that's another one wrapped up nicely," Brock said as he and Olivia made a second trip back to Belle Grove in twenty-four hours. They'd handed Sally over to be booked not just for her assistance in Danny's crimes, but also for the attempted murder of Olivia in her own home. Olivia knew she should probably be more shaken by the experience, but after all she'd faced in her life, facing a woman like Sally didn't give her much bother.

"We always get there in the end."

"We do. Though I'm sorry you had to go through something so awful in order for us to catch Sally…"

"Well, at least it keeps things interesting," Olivia said sarcastically. "I never imagined that one of my old classmates would turn out so badly. And the worst thing is that I still don't really remember her. She was so angry with me, Brock."

"High school politics... the bane of everyone's existence," Brock mused with a grim chuckle. "Still, at least you've got an interesting story for the next reunion..."

"I don't think I'll be going to one again... you never know what will happen," Olivia said with a shudder. "But I'm just glad it's over for good now. We don't have to spend our days looking over our shoulder anymore."

"I wouldn't be so sure," Brock said. "We can't forget that we still know at least one person on the run."

Olivia sighed. It seemed that no matter where they were or what they were thinking about, Yara's absence was a constant dark cloud over them. It was hard not to ask questions about it all, and now that their latest case was over, it was easy to slip back into worrying about it constantly. In her letters, she had warned of something incoming. Something the Gamemaster was planning. Olivia had no idea what that could be, and there was no way to guess. Again, she felt that she should be worried about what her future held. Something dark, no doubt.

But Olivia had felt a relative calm over her life in the last few weeks. The night at the hotel with Brock certainly hadn't hurt matters. She felt closer to him than ever before. The hints he'd made at marriage made her blush just thinking about it. She reached for Brock's hand as he drove.

"Well, for now, we've got to just try and enjoy life for what it is," she said. "I don't want to waste my time worrying about empty threats, about what could happen or not. Right?"

Brock smiled, brushing his thumb against her hand. "Right. We might get some peace for a while. Can't hurt to dream. And we've got the whole weekend ahead of us. We don't have any work to do..."

"Except for getting our locks changed," Olivia said with a shudder. "*Again.*"

"I think we're keeping Belle Grove's locksmith in business at this point," Brock said with a weary smile. "Still, it's better to be safe than sorry. And then we can relax. Okay?"

"Sounds perfect."

◦∞◦

Olivia heard the microwave ping and hurried over to get the warm, buttery popcorn out. It was their new Friday night tradition—a night in with a movie and snacks, considering that Belle Grove was too small to have its own movie theater. Olivia found the normalcy of the ritual to be comforting. After a big case, it was the best way she could think of to kick back and relax. They didn't need to frequent posh restaurants or get drunk in bars. Being in each other's company was Olivia's idea of a perfect date night.

She shook the bag of popcorn into a big bowl while Brock sighed behind her, flicking through the streaming service menu for something to watch.

"There's nothing on."

"That's not possible, Brock. It's not like when we were kids when there were three channels to pick from and if you didn't watch it live, you missed it. You've got thousands of shows to pick from."

"And yet there's nothing to watch. I swear they cancel every good show on here now," Brock said with a sigh. "I was loving that show we were watching…"

"The one about those girls who get stranded on the island? Feels a little too close to home these days, I'm almost glad it was canceled."

"No, not that one. The fantasy one where they all had cool powers and went on heists…"

"Oh yeah, that one. Strange, I thought that one was pretty popular. Who knows. If enough people get mad about it, they might start filming it again…"

"Now that would be nice. I never get anything I want," Brock said, pouting his lip. Olivia sniggered.

THE **HOUSEWIFE**

"Well, I salted the popcorn, so there's one thing you get. I don't know why you can't just stick with the sweet stuff."

"I guess you keep me sweet enough," Brock said with a grin.

Olivia rolled her eyes, but there was a blush settling on her cheeks.

Olivia sat beside Brock on the sofa and he pulled her in close to him, his arm snaking around her shoulder. Then, his hand strained for the bowl of popcorn on her lap, ruining the moment. She elbowed him in the ribs.

"Nope. Not today. Pick something to watch first before you start eating. If I've got to listen to you munching like a horse on popcorn then I've got to have background noise that'll keep me sane."

"*You* pick something. You've got good taste. Hence the reason you're dating me."

Olivia rolled her eyes again, a smile playing on her lips. She'd heard his lame jokes a million times by now, though hearing them never felt like a true chore. It simply felt familiar. And lately, it was moments like this that made her feel warm and fuzzy inside. Ever since their post-Valentine's date, she'd felt closer than ever to Brock. She was becoming accustomed to planning their future inside her head, preparing for a day when they were married together in a house they'd bought, working side by side each day to fight crime. It was a life that wasn't so far from what they had now, but the idea of the commitment enticed her. She had been engaged once before, but this was different. This time, she was certain it was what she wanted.

"Hurry up, I want to start the popcorn before it goes cold," Brock said, digging Olivia in the ribs. She tutted.

"Alright, I'm picking something, I'm picking something!"

But as she grabbed the remote from his hand to pick something, her phone began to ring. She sighed. It was her work phone, and therefore a call she couldn't ignore. She handed the bowl over to Brock.

"I've got to take this. You'd better not eat all of the popcorn while I'm gone," she warned Brock. He made a show of sitting on his hands, feigning innocence.

"I'll be good, I promise."

Olivia stood up and swept her phone off the table before answering it. The sooner she spoke to her boss, the sooner she could get back to movie night. For once, she was more than prepared to put work aside in favor of a quiet night in.

"Hi, Jonathan. Did you need something?"

"Something's come up, Olivia. I'm going to need you and Brock to come up to Washington. As fast as you can, please."

Olivia stopped in her tracks, frowning. Jonathan never called her by her first name. "Is it a case for us? So soon?"

"Not exactly. But it has to be you two. I need you here."

"Jonathan... is everything okay?"

"I'll explain when you get here. But as quick as you can, please. Time isn't my friend right now."

Olivia's heart stopped. She'd heard those words before... at least, she'd heard them flipped upside down. She took a steadying breath, not wanting to jump to conclusions. But something told her that Jonathan's call was not an ordinary one.

"We'll be right there," she said. She ended the call and rushed back through to the living room. Brock guiltily snatched his hand away from the bowl of popcorn, his cheeks puffed up like a hamster's pouch.

"I swear it was just one handful... that was quick. Are you alright? You look a little pale."

"We have to go," Olivia insisted. Brock frowned.

"But we were just about to start..."

"Brock, I'm being serious. I think Jonathan is in trouble. He wanted us to come up to the office. Right now."

Brock was on his feet in an instant, grabbing his coat and his keys. He didn't question her, simply trusting her urgency. They hastily locked up and headed to the car. Brock didn't ask what had rattled Olivia so much. He simply put his foot on the pedal and drove them up to Washington.

Olivia's heart hammered hard in her chest. Would they be too late? Was this what she thought it was? Fear for her boss made her mouth go dry. If her hunch was right, he could be dead at his desk by now. She didn't want to jump to conclusions, and yet her gut had never been wrong before.

THE **HOUSEWIFE**

It was late by the time they reached the city. The sky was dark and the streets were quiet enough that Brock could push the speed limit a little. When they arrived at their offices, there weren't many people hanging around. Was Jonathan alone in his office? Or had someone snuck in, unnoticed, to cause trouble?

There was only one way to find out.

Brock and Olivia quickly buzzed through security, quickly noted that things seemed as secure as ever, then approached their boss' office with their guns at hand. It felt like neither of them had breathed since Olivia had received the call.

The building seemed quiet. Olivia had to wonder if Jonathan had been placed under such duress that backup and building security wouldn't have been alerted.

But who could sneak into an FBI office and place a high-ranking special agent under such duress?

Was it the Gamemaster?

She nodded to Brock, whose hand found the handle to the door. He swung it open and Olivia burst inside.

Before her eyes was a scene so horrible that she forgot how to function. Sitting in his desk chair was Jonathan, his eyes wide with fear. Behind him stood Yara, a gun pressed to his head.

And behind her, Adeline Clarke, her gun to Yara's temple.

The Gamemaster.

"Hey, kids," Adeline said, her lips stretching over her teeth into a grotesque smile. "Fancy a game of Russian Roulette?"

AUTHOR'S NOTE

Thank you for reading *The Housewife*, the twelfth book in the Olivia Knight FBI Series. Your continued support has been the driving force behind the evolution of this series and the dynamic partnership of Olivia and Brock. We eagerly anticipate your company on the next exciting adventure with our beloved duo in 'Whispers at the Reunion'. While the idea of a family reunion might bring to mind thoughts of delicious food, clinking glasses, and cheerful gossip about loved ones, in this case, *some rumors can lead to murder...*

Our goal remains to provide you with the perfect escape into a world of non-stop excitement and action with every book. However, we can't do it alone! As indie writers, we don't have a big marketing budget or a massive following to help spread the word. That's where you come in! If you love the Olivia Knight series, please take a moment to leave us a review and tell your fellow book lovers about our latest installment. With your help, we can continue to bring you more thrilling adventures with Olivia and Brock, and make our mark in the world of crime fiction.

Thank you for your continued support, and we can't wait to take you on more thrilling adventures with the Olivia Knight FBI series!

By the way, if you find any typos, have suggestions, or just simply want to reach out to us, feel free to email us at egray@ellegraybooks.com

Your writer friends,
Elle Gray & K.S. Gray

CONNECT WITH ELLE GRAY

Loved the book? Don't miss out on future reads! Join my newsletter and receive updates on my latest releases, insider content, and exclusive promos. Plus, as a thank you for joining, you'll get a FREE copy of my book Deadly Pursuit!

Deadly Pursuit follows the story of Paxton Arrington, a police officer in Seattle who uncovers corruption within his own precinct. With his career and reputation on the line, he enlists the help of his FBI friend Blake Wilder to bring down the corrupt Strike Team. But the stakes are high, and Paxton must decide whether he's willing to risk everything to do the right thing.

Claiming your freebie is easy! Visit
https://dl.bookfunnel.com/513mluk159
and sign up with your email!

Want more ways to stay connected? Follow me on Facebook and Instagram or sign up for text notifications by texting "blake" to 844-552-1368. Thanks for your support and happy reading!

ALSO BY
ELLE GRAY

Blake Wilder FBI Mystery Thrillers

Book One - The 7 She Saw
Book Two - A Perfect Wife
Book Three - Her Perfect Crime
Book Four - The Chosen Girls
Book Five - The Secret She Kept
Book Six - The Lost Girls
Book Seven - The Lost Sister
Book Eight - The Missing Woman
Book Nine - Night at the Asylum
Book Ten - A Time to Die
Book Eleven - The House on the Hill
Book Twelve - The Missing Girls
Book Thirteen - No More Lies
Book Fourteen - The Unlucky Girl
Book Fifteen - The Heist
Book Sixteen - The Hit List
Book Seventeen - The Missing Daughter
Book Eighteen - The Silent Threat
Book Nineteen - A Code to Kill
Book Twenty - Watching Her

A Pax Arrington Mystery
Free Prequel - Deadly Pursuit
Book One - I See You
Book Two - Her Last Call
Book Three - Woman In The Water
Book Four - A Wife's Secret

Storyville FBI Mystery Thrillers
Book One - The Chosen Girl
Book Two - The Murder in the Mist
Book Three - Whispers of the Dead
Book Four - Secrets of the Unseen

A Sweetwater Falls Mystery
Book One - New Girl in the Falls
Book Two - Missing in the Falls
Book Three - The Girls in the Falls
Book Four - Memories of the Falls
Book Five - Shadows of the Falls
Book Six - The Lies in the Falls

ALSO BY
ELLE GRAY | K.S. GRAY

Olivia Knight FBI Mystery Thrillers
Book One - New Girl in Town
Book Two - The Murders on Beacon Hill
Book Three - The Woman Behind the Door
Book Four - Love, Lies, and Suicide
Book Five - Murder on the Astoria
Book Six - The Locked Box
Book Seven - The Good Daughter
Book Eight - The Perfect Getaway
Book Nine - Behind Closed Doors
Book Ten - Fatal Games
Book Eleven - Into the Night
Book Twelve - The Housewife

ALSO BY
ELLE GRAY | JAMES HOLT

The Florida Girl FBI Mystery Thrillers
Book One - The Florida Girl
Book Two - Resort to Kill
Book Three - The Runaway
Book Four - The Ransom

Printed in Great Britain
by Amazon